"I'm not safe here.

Garret reached for her hand. "I can't guarantee it, but I believe you're safe with me. For right now anyway."

"Then you're worried, too." They stepped onto the terrace that overlooked the river. "Do you know what's going on?"

"I don't believe your father died of natural causes," he confessed. "And then you show up in town and you're attacked at the newspaper and at your dad's house... It's starting to add up."

"To what?"

He sighed. "I'm worried, Megan. Worried that just knowing about it might put you in danger."

"I'm already in danger."

He gazed out at the river, questioning just how much to tell her. Wouldn't her father want Garret to keep her safe? Keep her alive?

Before he could decide what to do, she screamed.

"Garret, get down!"

Melody Carlson has worn many hats, from preschool teacher to political activist to senior editor. But most of all, she loves to write! She has published over two hundred books—with sales of over six million copies, and she has received the *RT Book Reviews* Lifetime Achievement Award. She and her husband have two grown sons and live in Sisters, Oregon, with their Labrador retriever, Audrey. They enjoy skiing, hiking and biking in the Cascade Mountains.

Books by Melody Carlson

Love Inspired Suspense

Perfect Alibi
No One to Trust
Against the Tide

AGAINST THE TIDE

MELODY CARLSON

 HARLEQUIN® LOVE INSPIRED® SUSPENSE

Recycling programs
for this product may
not exist in your area.

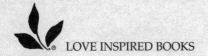 LOVE INSPIRED BOOKS

ISBN-13: 978-0-373-67774-0

Against the Tide

www.Harlequin.com

Printed in U.S.A.

Hear me when I call, O God of my righteousness:
thou hast enlarged me when I was in distress;
have mercy upon me, and hear my prayer.
—*Psalms* 4:1

ONE

Megan McCallister thought her emotions were under control by the time she reached Cape Perpetua on the Central Oregon Coast, but seeing the familiar newspaper office produced a dark well of sadness within her. Dad was gone. She slowed her car as she drove past the old shake-sided building, taking in a quick breath as she glimpsed the faded sign above the front door. The Perpetual Press. The building looked sad, almost like it, too, was grieving the loss of its owner.

This family-owned newspaper had survived the Great Depression, the recent recession and even the news-source domination of the internet. The weekly paper's old press machines would soon grind to a complete halt. Just like her father's life. She sighed, trying to grasp this. Was it only yesterday that Dad's fishing boat had gone down in the Pacific?

The sound of a blaring horn reminded her

that, thanks to Memorial Day weekend, Main Street was crawling with traffic. She needed to keep moving.

When had Cape Perpetua gone from being a sleepy fishing town to this bustling place? Parking her Prius about a block from the newspaper office, she blinked back tears and attempted to steady herself. *Just get through this. Do what needs to be done and move on. Buck up!* That was what her no-nonsense dad would tell her.

As Megan got out of the car, she could hear strains of music mixed with the sounds of jovial voices, happy folks out enjoying this unusually warm evening. Of course, she realized as she locked her car, the busyness of town was due to the holiday. These oblivious tourists had no idea that one of Cape Perpetua's heroes had died yesterday. Why should they?

Feeling conspicuously lonely, Megan averted her eyes from the out-of-towners as she hurried toward the office. She knew it was closed and locked up. But she still wanted to go inside, to look around and maybe, she hoped, to feel her dad's presence again. She unzipped her oversize purse, feeling around for the key.

The sound of a car's backfire made her jump, and that was when she noticed the sunset. Rose-colored light reflected on the river that flowed alongside the town, past the jetties, and into the ocean. *Red sky at night, sailors' delight...* The pretty image was blurred by her unshed tears as she dug for the key. It had to be there—she always kept it with her. To her relief, she felt the rounded oblong shape of the wooden fishing lure. Extracting it, she saw that it was still attached to the old-fashioned brass key. Unless Dad had changed the locks, and she felt certain he hadn't, this key should get her inside.

She paused for a moment in front of the office, staring up at the unimpressive single-story building. It all looked the same. The big front window and glass door, the grayed cedar shakes and white trim, which as usual needed painting, had not changed. In fact, little had changed since her great-grandfather built the humble structure almost a hundred years ago. Dad had been planning a centennial celebration for the upcoming spring. That probably wouldn't happen now. Or if it did, it would be in the hands of a new owner.

She fumbled to get her key into the keyhole. She knew it was the right key, but it refused to slide inside the lock. She bent down to see better in the dimming light, making sure that the dead bolt lock hadn't been changed. But it looked the same. So, once again, she shoved the key in, but it only went partway before it stuck. In complete frustration, she kicked the door with her foot. "Come on!"

"Excuse me?" A deep voice gave her a start.

Megan turned to see a dark-haired man standing behind her. Several inches taller and dressed casually in faded jeans and a dark blue jacket, he was peering at her with what seemed a suspicious expression.

"What?" She stepped back from the stranger, bumping into the glass door as she held up her key like a defensive weapon—a trick she'd picked up while living in the big city these past seven years. But the yellow wooden fish lure with its buggy eyes swung back and forth as if to mock her. As if to say she was really a wimp.

"Excuse me." His voice grew warmer. "But the newspaper office is closed in the evenings."

"I *know* it's closed," she said in a slightly terse tone.

"But you're kicking the door?" His brow creased.

She waved her key under his nose as if to make a point. "This is my *family's* newspaper," she declared. "The stupid key isn't working."

He leaned forward, peering curiously at her in the light coming from the nearby streetlamp. "Hey, are you Rory's daughter?"

"Did you know my father?"

"I did." He slowly nodded as he looked at her with what now seemed compassionate eyes. "And I knew you, too." He stuck out his hand. "I'm Garret Larsson. And you're Megan. Megan McCallister."

"Garret Larsson?" She gingerly shook his hand, trying to remember why the name rang a bell.

"I was a couple years ahead of you in school. I doubt you'd even remember me." He grinned. And she had to admit it was a handsome grin. "Maybe you recall my grandparents, though. They owned Larsson's Marina."

"Oh, yeah." She nodded. "I remember now." The truth was she only vaguely remembered this guy. But she did remember Dad had kept his boat at that marina.

"I'm so sorry about your dad," Garret told her. "Such a huge loss for everyone. But especially you."

"Thanks." She held up her key again. "I just wanted to go inside—to, you know—just to, well…you know." She felt the lump returning to her throat. *Don't cry, don't cry,* she told herself.

"Yeah." He nodded sadly. "I know."

"I guess I'm still trying to absorb the news," she confessed. "I mean, it's so hard to believe. How could my dad, the indomitable Rory McCallister, have drowned while fishing? It just doesn't make sense."

Garret nodded. He didn't speak, but his eyes

seemed understanding. She felt his empathy, probably the reason she continued talking.

"I checked the weather on the internet last night," she blurted, "and it sounded like it had been a beautiful day here—calm seas, no wind, no fog. No hazards or warnings of any kind."

Garret rubbed his chin with a thoughtful expression. "A perfect Fisherman's Thursday."

"You know about Fisherman's Thursday?"

"Sure. The paper comes out on Wednesdays, and Rory celebrates by going fishing on Thursdays. Rather, he used to." He cleared his throat.

Megan blinked. "Yeah. That's right." Garret really did seem to know a lot about her dad. And although that seemed slightly odd, it was also a relief. She'd been so eager to talk to someone—*anyone*—who knew her dad. Someone who knew about what had happened yesterday. Who could commiserate with her and perhaps answer some questions. She had many.

And so, like liquid from an uncorked bottle, they poured out. "I just don't understand," she began. "How could his boat have gone down? And on such a nice clear day? It makes no sense. Even if his boat had developed a mechanical problem out there, which seems unlikely. I mean, my dad was meticulous about his boat engines. And safety, too. So why would his boat go down? Even if he did have a problem, why wouldn't he have radioed someone? Or sent out a distress signal? And why didn't someone go out there and rescue him?"

"Maybe he didn't have time to send a signal."

"Yeah, that's what Lieutenant Conrad suggested." She pulled out a tissue to dab a straying tear. "He's the one who called last night with the bad news. He suggested that while Dad was out fishing by himself he might've suffered a heart attack. He said the coroner is doing an autopsy, but they don't expect to find anything beyond natural causes. But that still doesn't explain his boat going down, does it?" She shoved the tissue back into her purse. "I mean, on a clear, calm day how does a boat just sink?"

"It can happen." He pursed his lips as if weighing his words. "For instance, if your dad did suffer a heart attack or stroke or was somehow incapacitated, there'd be no one at the helm. The boat would start drifting. Even on a calm sea, there's a tide. There are waves. Even what's known as a rogue wave, although I hadn't heard of any yesterday. But with no one steering, a boat can get rocked and tossed. It might even be rolled and then it would take on water, capsize and sink." He frowned. "It happens. Even in good weather the ocean is the ocean—it can be unmerciful on a disabled boat."

"Oh…" She honestly hadn't considered any of that.

"I heard from a friend in the coast guard that they spotted the debris while doing a routine flyover in the helicopter yesterday. From the air, the scene had all the earmarks of a sunken vessel. Swirling gas and oil, miscellaneous items from the boat—ice chests, flotation devices, that remained on the surface while the boat went down." His brow creased. "And they discovered your dad only a mile or two away—thanks to his orange life vest."

Megan felt fresh tears filling her eyes as she envisioned this scene. "Well, thanks for telling me. I—I still can't quite believe it."

He nodded with a troubled brow. "I've had a hard time accepting it, too. The only reasonable theory seems to be heart attack or stroke. Something instant. That makes sense."

"Maybe it makes sense to you," she declared hotly. "But Dad grew up fishing this ocean. Just like his father and grandfather before him. People always said the McCallister men had seawater in their veins. But they were never careless. They respected the changeable weather. They took red flag warnings seriously, always kept their radios tuned, knew the tide schedules almost intuitively and, until yesterday, none had been lost at sea."

He simply pointed to the key still dangling from her hand. "How about I help you with that?"

She shrugged as she handed it over. "If you think you can."

To her surprise, he spit on it. "Sorry about that," he said as he worked it into the keyhole. "But it usually works. Not as good as WD-40 or even a chalk stick, but these old locks can get cranky. You know how the salt air can corrode." And just like that, he turned the key and the door creaked open. He removed the key, wiped it on the back of his jeans and handed it back with a sheepish smile.

"Thanks." She dropped it into her purse. "And thanks for listening to me." She sighed. "I didn't mean to go on like that."

"No problem." He tipped his head toward the slightly opened door. "Want any company in there?"

"No," she said briskly. "I need to do this alone."

He nodded. "I figured."

She thanked him again and then, pushing the door fully open, she suddenly felt a bit reluctant about going inside. Was she truly ready for this? Maybe she didn't really want to be alone. She turned to see Garret crossing the street, waving to someone on the other side as he headed for Beulah's Café. She glanced over to the bay, which was now dark with the sun fully down. Several boats were cruising slowly through the calm water with running lights on. Normally, this made a pretty picture, one that she used to enjoy. But tonight it just made her sad.

She took in a deep breath, knowing what she had to do. She needed to go inside the newspaper office, to walk through the building—with no one else there. Partly to say goodbye to her dad, and partly to prepare herself for what she knew must be done in the next few days. The closing of the newspaper. As painful as it would be, she just needed to get it over with.

With only the streetlight to illuminate the small entry area, she could see Barb's tidy reception desk still sat across from the door; the three orange vinyl chairs in the waiting area stood in a row with the stodgy little coffee table and its usual neat stack of this week's paper; the faded fake ficus tree still stood in the corner—just like a time warp. Even the smell was the same, a combination of ink, paper and dust.

Megan flicked on the fluorescent overhead lights, causing the scene to pop at her in a way that twisted her heart even more tightly. It was all still here—just like she remembered it—but Dad was gone and it would be her unpleasant job to shut the place down. She didn't look forward to that meeting. She'd need to get her bearings to prepare the dismal announcement. Without her dad to run it, the paper would need to close. It would be the end of an era.

As she walked past the staff desks, she wished for another way. If only *The Perpetual Press* wasn't so old-fashioned. But Dad hadn't listened to her encouragement to offer an online news source for additional revenue. He had stubbornly insisted on running the paper the way his dad and grandpa had done. He hadn't even owned a computer. She paused to remember the clickity-clack of his old typewriter—and then she froze at the sound of something else. She was not alone!

The scuffling noise came from somewhere in the back of the building. Was Arthur here? The old print operator sometimes liked to clean the press at night when no one else was around to complain about the smelly emollients he used. But the door to the printing room was closed and she spied no ribbon of light beneath the door.

"Arthur?" she called out as she reached for the doorknob. But before she could open it, she heard fast footsteps behind her.

"Arthur?" With a racing heart, she spun around. In the same instant a dark figure lunged toward her. She let out a scream as he tackled her to the floor. Swinging her fists and kicking her legs, Megan screamed at the top of her lungs as she fought her attacker. But bigger and stronger, he soon had her facedown on the old pine floor. Pressing her head down onto the boards with one hand, he used his knee to pin her tightly, pushing so hard she could barely breathe and felt her ribs were about to snap.

"Who are you?" she gasped with what little breath was left. "What are you do—"

"Shut up!" he said. Then he slapped her across the side of the head—so hard that her head smacked into the floor and she could almost see stars. The only thing she could do was pray.

TWO

Garret hadn't wanted to leave Rory's daughter like that. She'd looked so lost and alone, standing in front of the newspaper office. With her long auburn hair and somber eyes, she reminded him of a sad little girl. Troubled and fragile and broken. Yet, he could tell Megan was trying to appear strong. Garret remembered Rory's high praise for his only child, portraying her as a smart, strong, independent young woman.

Garret knew from his frequent chats with Rory that Megan had gotten a job with a big Seattle newspaper a couple years after finishing college, and that she'd diligently worked her way up to a good position. Rory had been extremely proud of her, but he'd also missed his girl. And it was no secret that Rory had hoped Megan would eventually return to Cape Perpetua to take over the family newspaper. "That way I can go fishing whenever I like," he'd joked to everyone at his recent birthday get-together. Now it was too late.

As Garret entered Beulah's Café, he was still thinking about Megan. Wishing he'd stuck around long enough to walk her through the deserted building. He knew she needed someone to talk to. She had so many questions. Many of the same ones he'd been wrestling with since yesterday. But he also knew that she needed this time alone. She had to process Rory's death in her own way, on her own terms. Just like Garret had done last night down at the docks where Rory used to keep his boat. It made sense that Megan would tell her father goodbye in the newspaper office. And yet the idea of her alone over there made him uneasy. As he looked around the crowded café, he had to admit there was a lot in this town that was making him uneasy.

Going toward an unoccupied stool at the counter, Garret waved to Jeanie as she emerged from the kitchen with a burger basket in each hand.

"Hey, handsome," the middle-aged waitress called out to him as she set the baskets in front of two teen girls. "How ya doing?"

"I'm okay," he said as he took a seat.

"What can I get you?"

"Just a bowl of chowder," he told her. "When you're not too busy, that is."

"You got it, honey." Jeanie waved toward the door. "Hey, Barry," she called out warmly to a newcomer. "How's the crabbing today?"

"Not bad." Barry took the stool next to Garret. "Hey, man." He slapped him on the back. "What's up?"

"Not much." Garret smiled at the burly fisherman.

"So…who was that pretty gal I saw you yapping with across the street?" Barry had a twinkle in his eye. "A real looker, that one." He playfully elbowed Garret. "You got yourself a woman we don't know about?"

"That's Rory's daughter," Garret said somberly. "Megan McCallister."

"Oh." Barry's smile faded. "So how's she doing?"

"Not so good."

"Hard losing a parent." Barry picked up a plastic-encased menu, wiping it with his sleeve. "Lost my old man last year. But he was in bad shape with his diabetes. And a lot older than Rory, too."

"Yeah." Garret nodded. "Megan wasn't ready to see her dad go yet."

"I was surprised to see the newspaper office

open tonight." Barry tipped his head toward the front window.

"It's not open," Garret corrected him. "Megan just wanted to go inside and look around some. No one else is there."

Barry looked slightly perplexed. "Wonder why she left the back open if she's there by herself."

"What're you talking about?" Garret felt uneasy.

"Well, town's so busy that I parked behind the newspaper. That's when I noticed the back door ajar. Figured someone was working late. But it seemed kinda odd, this being a Friday, and with Rory just passing away."

Garret frowned. "You saying the back door was open?"

"Yep." Barry nodded. "Propped with a trash can."

Maybe it was nothing. Or maybe it wasn't. But as Garret slowly stood, he knew he needed to find out. "Hey, Jeanie, hold off on that chowder for now. I need to go check on something." And without saying another word, he hurried outside. It was possible he was just overreacting. Or looking for an excuse to talk to Megan again. But it didn't really matter. As he jogged across the street, he knew, even if he was being melodramatic, there was no way he wasn't going to find out why that back door was open.

With her attacker's knee still painfully pressed into the middle of her back, Megan could barely breathe, let alone speak. Not that she knew what to say, besides plead for her life. With the side of her head flattened against the gritty floor, she could see, just barely, from one eye. And unless she imagined it, she detected a bluish light on the wood plank floor. Like the light from a cell phone.

In the next instant she could hear what sounded like the thug above her sending a text message. Really? Who was he texting and why? "Are you on your phone?" she gasped.

He swore at her, pressing his knee down even harder. She tried to think of reasons a thug would text someone while pinning down his victim. Was it possible he was asking someone for instructions—like what he should do with her?

As impossible as it seemed, she suddenly wondered if he might be a security guard. Perhaps he'd assumed she was an intruder and he was simply doing his job. Although it seemed unlikely, it was preferable to the alternative.

Still messing with his phone, the thug eased his knee slightly from her back, allowing her to take in a bigger breath and speak. "I'm Rory

McCallister's daughter. I didn't break in. My father owns this—"

"Your father's dead!" he growled, pressing his knee so hard into her midsection that she imagined her ribs cracking.

With him still distracted with his phone, she strained to look at him from the corner of her eye. He had on black jeans and a black hooded sweatshirt. The hood was pulled low over his face, but she could see that his skin was pale. Ghostly pale. And pock-marked. He looked to be in his twenties. She didn't recognize him. She saw him slip his phone into his sweatshirt pocket and suddenly he struggled to reach something from behind him. Was he trying to extract something from a back pocket or maybe from his belt? A firearm perhaps? The pressure from his knee eased up as he worked to get whatever it was he was looking for.

"Why are you doing this?" she said quietly, hoping to reason with him. "You don't even know me and—"

Swearing at her, he used his free hand to smack the back of her head again. This creep was no security guard.

"Please, let me go," she begged. "Please."

Just then, she heard the swishing sound of metal, almost like a sword being extracted from a sheath. Probably the weapon he was trying to get out of his belt. From the corner of her eye, she saw a metallic flash and when he raised his arm in the air, she could see what appeared to be a large hunting knife in his hand.

"Please, don't," she cried. "Whatever you're about to do—*stop*!" She tried to think of a way to dissuade him. "I have money! In my purse!" she shrieked. "You can have it all and I can pay you more if you let me go. My father just died—I'll have even more money." An exaggeration, yes, but she was desperate. "Please, don't kill me. I'll give you whatever—"

He swore again as he grabbed a fistful of her long hair. Jerking her head back so hard she thought her neck would snap, he let out a low, guttural chuckle, so evil-sounding that her flesh crawled in raw terror. This monster would enjoy murdering her. She knew it was hopeless. He planned to slit her throat.

But she would not go down without a fight.

THREE

Exhausted after what she now realized was a futile struggle, Megan racked her brain for another way out. She tried to catch her breath as she braced herself for her assailant's next move, but a noise from the front of the building distracted him. Knowing such an action could give him reason to finish her off, she decided to take the chance, anyway. With what little air remained in her lungs and her last ounce of energy, she let out a shrill scream for help.

Her cries were answered by the fast clomp of footsteps. Someone was running this way, and in the next moment she felt the weight of her attacker's knee lifted from her. Gasping for breath, she spun away and, scrambling across the gritty floor, she ducked under a staff writer's desk. Cowering in the knee-space, she listened as a scuffle ensued. She wished she had her phone, but her purse was still on Barb's desk. And she wondered about her rescuer. Who was he? And how could she help him?

As she felt around the top of the desk, hoping for a paperweight or something to use as a weapon, she heard the sounds of running footsteps and spied both men racing toward the back of the building, followed by the slamming of the back door—then silence.

Still shaking from head to toe, she could barely think straight. What had just happened? And why? As she hurried up front to get her purse and phone, she begged God to help whoever it was that had suddenly jumped into the fray. She'd just reached the front of the building when she heard footsteps in the rear—running toward her.

"Hello?" a male voice yelled. "Where are you?"

Megan was afraid to answer as she ducked behind Barb's big reception desk, wishing she'd grabbed her phone. Who was it? The man who wanted to slit her throat? Or the one who'd chased him away? Or could it be someone else? Someone connected to her attacker? Hadn't he texted someone, a cohort perhaps?

"Megan?" the man yelled from the center of the building. "Are you okay?"

Still feeling shocked and confused, Megan tried to think. Who was calling for her by name?

"It's Garret Larsson," the voice declared. "Are you still here, Megan?"

She barely poked her head above the desk, peeking over the edge to be certain it was Garret. "It's you!" She stood in relief, trying to control her shaking knees.

"Are you okay?" Garret hurried toward her.

"Yeah, I guess, just shaken." She brushed the dust from the front of her shirt and pants as she looked at him. "What happened?"

"That's what I want to know." He took her hand, leading her to a chair by the front door, helping her to sit down.

"What happened to that—that guy?" She heard the tremor in her voice.

"I chased him, nearly caught him." He paused for a breath. "But I lost him after a couple blocks. I just called 911. Police are on their way." He sat next to her, looking intently into her face. "What happened? Tell me."

She took in a steadying breath, trying to appear calm, but knowing that she was close to breaking. "I heard someone in here. I thought it was Arthur. He cleans the press at night sometimes. I went to see." She shuddered. "And then this—this guy jumped me, pinned me down. He—he had a knife." She felt herself shaking uncontrollably as she remembered that feeling of total helplessness.

"You're probably in shock." Garret removed his fleece jacket, slipping it over her shoulders. "Just take some slow, deep breaths."

"Thanks," she muttered, comforted by the warmth and his words. And taking his advice, she breathed slowly and deeply, reminding herself she was a strong woman. "It all happened so fast. So frightening. I just don't understand. Why did he want to kill me?"

"I don't know." Garret shook his head with a serious expression.

She studied him more closely now. In the bright light of the office, she could see that his dark brown hair was wavy and long enough to curl around his ears. And his eyes, a rich shade of teal-blue, looked very concerned.

"I'm so thankful you came when you did." She shuddered to think what might've happened if he hadn't shown up right then. "What made you come back here?"

"A friend mentioned seeing the back door open. It didn't sound right to me. I wanted to make sure you were okay."

"Th-thank you." Her voice cracked with emotion. "I—I don't know what I'd have done if you—if you—" It felt like the dam had broken as she crumbled into sobs.

Garret slipped a comforting arm around her shoulders, holding her closer. "It's okay," he said gently. "You have the right to cry. You've been through a lot."

She leaned into him, letting her emotions and tears flow freely, until she finally started to feel self-conscious. As always, she wanted to be strong, in control. She was Rory McCallister's daughter, after all. Sitting up straighter, she squared her shoulders. "It's just that—well, first Dad is gone. And then *this* happens. It's all so shocking." She wiped her wet cheeks with the backs of her hands. "So frightening. I feel so confused."

He was still looking intently into her eyes. "That's not surprising. You've been through quite an ordeal. And you could've been killed."

Her hand went to her throat as she remembered that moment when she expected to die. "I was so scared. I've never been that scared before. I still don't know why he wanted to kill me. I even offered him money to let me go."

"Really?" Garret frowned. "And he wasn't interested?"

"No." She shook her head. "Isn't that odd? Most criminals are looking for cash." She took in another deep breath, hearing the sounds of sirens approaching. "How'd he get in?"

"Looks like he used a crowbar to jimmy the back door."

He nodded toward the front windows, where

red and blue lights were flashing outside. "The police are here." With his arm still around her shoulders, he helped her stand, guiding her toward the front door.

By the time they got outside, a couple of police cruisers were double parking and to her relief, Lieutenant Michael Conrad was getting out of the first one. Although he was a few years younger than her dad, the two men had been good friends for as long as Megan could remember. Lieutenant Conrad was a good guy.

"Megan McCallister," he exclaimed as he approached the building. "Is that really you?"

Megan confirmed this as they shook hands, then Garret quickly explained about the criminal getting away and the route he may have taken.

"The dispatcher already sent someone that way," Lieutenant Conrad told him. "So you interrupted a robbery in process?" he asked Megan.

"I thought that was it," she told him, "but when I offered him money to let me go, he didn't seem interested."

"He threatened her life," Garret said solemnly.

Megan explained about the knife and how Garret had arrived just in time. But because a curious crowd was gathering, Lieutenant Conrad urged them to go back inside.

"The perpetrator broke in through the back door," Garret explained as they went inside.

Lieutenant Conrad paused, calling out to the other officers to check out the back of the building.

"Did you get a look at his face?" he asked her as they entered the building. "Can you identify him?"

"He was Caucasian, looked like he was in his twenties. Bad complexion. And he was dressed in all black. Black jeans and a black hooded sweatshirt."

"Height? Weight?"

"Maybe six foot?" Megan said with uncertainty.

"He was a little shorter than me, so six foot sounds about right," Garret confirmed.

"Medium build," Megan suggested.

"Did you see a vehicle?" Lieutenant Conrad asked Garret.

Garret shook his head. "I lost him while he was on foot. Those dark clothes were hard to see at night. I didn't see a vehicle speeding away, but the town's pretty busy. Lots of traffic out there."

"Let me get this info out." Lieutenant Conrad pulled out his phone and, stepping away, began to relay what they'd told him.

Megan glanced out the window, looking at the blur of flashing emergency lights and the busy street. "Do you think the break-in was related to the holiday weekend?" she ventured quietly.

Although she didn't really think so. Why would a random burglar be so intent on killing her?

Garret frowned. "Hard to say."

"I do remember how our little town could get sort of wild during tourist season." She knew she was just making idle chatter now, trying to wrap her head around all that had happened and feeling pretty lost.

Lieutenant Conrad finished his call and returned to them. "They'll be watching for the perpetrator all over town," he assured them. And then he asked a few more questions. They both answered them as best they could.

"And you feel certain he intended to kill you?"

She just nodded. "His knife was ready. Garret got here just in time."

"Could you see if anything was stolen?" Lieutenant Conrad asked. "Anything missing?"

"I didn't have a chance to look around, but it's not like there's much to steal in here," she said. "Dad never kept much cash in the office. And that would be in Barb's desk up in front. Besides, the guy didn't seem interested in money." She pointed to the other end of the building. "But it looks like he could've been in my dad's office. The light's on in there."

"Did you look in there yet?"

"No, not yet." Megan swallowed hard. That was why she'd come here tonight…to sit in Dad's old leather chair, to breathe in the dusty, musty air, to feel his presence one more time. She bit her lip, determined not to cry again.

"How about we take a look around," Lieutenant Conrad said as he led the way back there.

As they walked past the area where she'd been pinned on the floor, Megan felt a little weak-kneed and off balance. But Garret, seeming to sense this, put his hand on her back as if to steady her.

Lieutenant Conrad used his elbow to nudge the door open, warning them not to touch anything. But to Megan's dismay, the office looked nothing like it should've looked. It was as if someone had turned it upside down. All the drawers in the desk and file cabinet were opened and dumped out. Even the pictures had been removed from the wall, many of them lying in broken shards on the floor. The place was a shambles.

Megan's hand flew to her mouth. She was unable to speak or even think. Why would anyone do this? What could he have been looking for?

"What about your dad's computer?" Lieutenant Conrad asked her.

"Computer?" She made a choked laugh. "Dad never used a computer. I thought everyone in Cape Perpetua knew that."

"I know Rory hated electronics, but how did he run a newspaper without one?" Lieutenant

Conrad carefully poked around beneath a pile of papers on the desk.

"Dad's writers had computers. But he always insisted on hard copies. For everything—from obits to advertisements. He ran this paper the same way his dad and grandpa had."

Garret nodded. "Yeah, I thought that was pretty cool."

"I used to give him a bad time about wasting trees," she said sadly. "And he would just remind me that they were a renewable resource."

"What do you think the perpetrator was looking for?" Lieutenant Conrad asked her.

"I have no idea." Megan slowly shook her head. She didn't like to be such a weakling, but this whole thing was making her feel sick to her stomach. "I—I think I need some air," she said quietly. "Please excuse me."

She rushed out of the office, trying to compose herself. If losing Dad wasn't hard enough, why did someone have to do this—to break in and make such a big mess? And to threaten her life? It all felt like such a cruel violation...nothing made sense.

"Are you okay?" Garret joined her out by the staff writers' desks.

"Not really." She scowled. "I'm scared and I'm angry...and I'm exhausted." She sat down on one of the desks and folded her arms in front of her in exasperation. "I hardly slept after the call about Dad late last night. Then I went into work early this morning. Just to manage some things so I could get out of there. And then I drove nearly nine hours to get here." She pursed her lips, willing herself not to cry again. "I—I just want to go home."

"To your dad's place?" he asked gently.

"Yeah." She sniffed, desperately trying not to fall apart again.

"Do you think you'll be safe out there?" Garret made a concerned frown. "I mean, considering what just happened here. Aren't you worried?"

Lieutenant Conrad was coming out of the office with his cell phone in hand again. "I've got a couple more officers on their way," he told them. "We'll go over everything in here and then secure the place before we leave." He peered at Megan. "Feel free to go. You look pretty worn out."

"I'll get you a key, Lieutenant Conrad," she said. "Thanks."

"You're old enough to call me by my first name, Megan." His smile looked sad.

"Okay. Thanks… Michael."

She sighed as they walked to the front of the building, still trying to wrap her head around all that had happened, realizing once again how she might've been dead right now. They could've held a double funeral—her and Dad. An involuntary shiver ran down her spine as she picked up her purse from Barb's desk. Then, remembering Michael would need to lock up, she opened the top drawer of Barb's desk and, just like always, the spare key was in the far right-hand corner, right beneath the paper clips.

"Please keep me in the loop about this." She removed one of her business cards from a side pocket of her purse, handing it over with the key. "This has my cell number on it."

"Thanks." Michael slipped them into his pocket. "I'll be in touch."

As they stood at the door, Megan noticed what appeared to be a recently installed security system panel. "This is new to me." She pointed to the sleek stainless keypad.

"Was it activated when you arrived?" Michael asked her. "Did you have to put in a passcode?"

"No. I don't even know the passcode." She frowned. "Dad always made fun of these devices. He used to brag about how safe this town was. Sometimes he didn't even lock the door."

"Well, times have changed," Michael told her. "I'll call the security service and see if I can get them to activate it again when I leave. That might help ward off any more break-ins."

"Yeah."

"And I'll send the passcode to your phone in case you need to get back in here tomorrow."

"Thanks, that'll be helpful."

"I wonder why it wasn't set," Garret said as he and Megan stepped outside. "Of course, the staff was probably upset and distracted by the news of Rory's death. Maybe they forgot."

"That makes sense." Megan nodded numbly. She felt she was walking through a weird dream. Like none of this was real. But outside, as the cool sea air washed over her face, smelling like a familiar mixture of rotten eggs and dead fish, signaling that the tide was low, she suddenly knew that this was all real. Painfully real. She was home in Cape Perpetua, and Dad was dead.

"I'm parked over there." She pointed to the side street. "But you don't have to walk me—"

"I *want* to," he insisted.

As she turned the corner, she noticed that the traffic in town had thinned considerably. Hers was the only car parked on the side street now.

"That's not your car, is it?" Garret pointed at the white Prius parked beneath a streetlamp.

"Yeah, that's it." As she walked, she dug in the bottom of her purse, trying to feel her car keys.

"Check out your tires," he said in an odd tone.

She paused from her key search, peering down at her tires. "What?" She moved closer to see what was wrong. "They're flat!"

Garret knelt down, using his own car key to poke into a gash on the side of her car's front tire. "Slashed."

"What is wrong with people?" she demanded hotly. "Why would someone do this? What has happened to this town?" Hot, angry tears were filling her eyes.

"I don't know." Garret just shook his head. "Either it was just a random act of meanness—or someone really doesn't like you."

Despite her resolve not to shed more tears, it was too late, they were coming—fast and furious. As she dug through her purse for a tissue, she wanted to scream and shout—and punch something. This was all just too much. First her dad died. Then she was nearly murdered. And the newspaper office was broken into and Dad's office trashed. And now her tires were slashed. What had she done to deserve this? More disturbing, what was next?

FOUR

Still wearing Garret's fleece jacket, Megan attempted to calm herself as she sat in his SUV in front of the newspaper office. Garret had gone back inside to tell Michael about the slashed tires. But suddenly she felt uneasy about sitting out here alone—where a killer could be lurking around the next corner. She slumped down in the seat, hitting the auto-lock button on the door. And, with her phone in hand, she kept a wary eye on the people moving along Main Street.

At close to eleven o'clock, the town had quieted down some, leaving only the boisterous barhoppers still out and about—the usual mix of out-of-towners, fishermen and young, antsy locals. The late-night activity was somewhat reassuring. She felt a little less alone.

Just the same, Megan was relieved to see Garret emerge from the newspaper office. She watched him with stealthy admiration as he strode over to the driver's side of his SUV. But when he couldn't open his door, she felt embarrassed. Releasing the auto-lock, she apologized as he climbed inside.

"I'm glad you did that," he told her. "After I went inside, I felt uneasy about leaving you out here by yourself. Michael suspects your attacker is probably long gone by now, but you never know. Can't be too safe." He started the ignition.

As Garret drove them through town, Megan continued trying to compose herself. She hated feeling like such a basket case. She normally considered herself to be a pragmatic person, not overly emotional. Journalists couldn't afford to be. Yet the slashed tires had pushed her over the edge. Her heart was still pounding in fury, and it was hard to calm down.

Still, she reminded herself, tires could be replaced. Her insurance might even cover the cost. And her dad's office could be cleaned up and put back together again. Her dad...well, there was nothing to be done about that, except to remember him for all the good he'd brought into her life. He would want her to do that. And, really, she should be thankful to still be alive.

"How are you doing?" Garret asked quietly.

"I'm trying to get it together," she confessed.

"I'm not used to being this emotional or out of control."

"Under the circumstances, it seems pretty natural."

She felt surprised when he turned on his signal to turn onto Rawlins Road. "So you know where you're going?"

"Yeah, sure. I've been to your dad's before."

She studied his profile as he drove. Firm chin, fairly straight nose, except for a slight bump, almost like it had been broken before, high forehead. Garret Larsson was very handsome. She didn't remember him being this good-looking back in high school. But to be fair, she barely remembered him at all. She knew about late bloomers. Those guys who slipped under the popularity radar in high school, but turned out to be pretty cool later on. She suspected that Garret was one of those.

"So you were obviously acquainted with my dad?" she said quietly.

"More than just acquainted. We were pretty good friends."

"You were *friends* with my dad?" She peered curiously at him, trying to imagine that. "So how did this friendship come about exactly? I mean, considering the gap in your ages, I'm a little confused."

"Rory kept his boat at my marina," Garret told her.

"Oh, yeah. The marina your grandparents owned."

"I started to manage it right after my grandpa died. It was too much for my grandma by then. She needed help."

"How long ago was that?"

"Five or six years. The place was pretty run-down. Mostly because my grandpa got too old to keep it up. So I started doing some renovations. Then my grandma passed on, too. Anyway, I inherited the marina and cabins and everything."

"And that's how you met my dad."

"Yeah. Sometimes we went out on the ocean together."

"You fished with my dad?" This spoke well of Garret. Her dad wouldn't fish with just anyone.

"Yeah. Sometimes. But your dad liked going out alone, too."

"I know. I wish he hadn't done that yesterday."

Garret sighed. "Me, too. I never like seeing anyone going out on the ocean by himself. I prefer the buddy system."

"I used to go fishing with him. After I left for college, I nagged him not to go alone, even if it was pointless. No one could tell Rory McCallister what to do."

"Yeah, but whenever I saw him going out

on his own, if I was free, I'd just invite myself along. He never seemed to mind."

Megan studied Garret closely. "Dad must've really liked you." And this was no exaggeration. Dad had been picky about fishing buddies. Stubborn and picky and opinionated. Still, how she would miss him!

Megan could feel herself slipping into an emotional tailspin again. She knew it was time to lighten the subject. If that was even possible. "So you and my dad were fishing friends... For some reason I can't quite see it." Just then she remembered something Dad had said about his "young fishing buddy." "Hey, you're not Tangler, are you?"

Garret chuckled. "That'd be me."

"Tangler? How'd you get that name?"

"That's what your dad called me when we first met. He saw me taking out a bunch of inexperienced fishermen—not my favorite thing to do, by the way, but these city boys booked a trip and I had to take them."

"Naturally."

"Well, these dudes didn't know a rod from a reel or a salmon from a halibut. Your dad was working on his boat while I was trying to get them loaded into mine and we must've looked like a floating circus." He laughed.

"But what does that have to do with your nickname?"

"Tangler is what a good fisherman calls an inexperienced angler. Because he's always getting his line tangled up. Tangled plus angler equals Tangler. Get it? Anyway, it stuck."

She almost smiled to remember how her dad could be such a tease at times. She would miss that, too. The lump in her throat was back, getting bigger as Garret turned down the unpaved road to her dad's house—the same house she'd grown up in. It was like she expected to see Dad there, standing on the front porch, cheerfully waving them inside, telling them he had tuna on the grill and a pitcher of homemade lemonade in the fridge.

"I admired Rory a lot," Garret said solemnly as they bumped along the rutted sandy road shared by a handful of neighbors. "I looked up to him like a father figure."

"Your parents were divorced, weren't they?" As soon as she said this, she regretted it. "I'm sorry," she said quickly. "It's none of my business. But you know how nosy reporters can be."

"It's okay. And it's true, my parents did divorce. A messy divorce, too. Fortunately, I had my grandparents and the marina to fill the void after my parents went their separate ways."

"It still must've been hard." She sighed. "My mom and dad divorced, too."

"According to Rory, they handled theirs in a fairly civilized way."

"Right." She wasn't so sure about that.

"Anyway, your dad was a good friend to me." Garret's voice was laced in sadness.

Megan looked out the window, seeing the dark glistening strip of ocean out past the few houses that lined this portion of the bluff. "I wish I'd taken more time off work—to come down here to visit more. I'm afraid I've let my career take over my life."

"Your dad was proud of you, Megan. He loved that you were working for a big Seattle paper. I know he missed you, but he did understand."

"I know." She sighed. "He always encouraged me to chase my dreams."

"And did you find them?"

She shrugged. "I thought so at first. To be honest, I'm not so sure now. It gets to feeling like a rat race out there. Not like life here in Cape Perpetua." Talk about an understatement.

Garret was turning into the sandy driveway now. It was hard to see the house in the darkness, but something about this scene didn't feel quite right. Probably the fact that her dad was missing from the picture. It was strange to see the house so dark. No glowing windows, no porch light, nothing. The house looked sad and lonely, as if it knew its owner was not coming home.

"Thanks for the ride," she told Garret as he stopped the SUV. She suddenly felt glum about parting ways with him. He'd been such a comfort tonight and it felt like they'd actually started to get acquainted. But now it was over.

"You're welcome. But don't think you're getting rid of me that easily." He was already getting out of the SUV. He hurried around, removing her baggage from the back, then joining her as she got out. "Let's make sure everything is okay here first."

"It, uh, looks okay to me." She tried to sound more confident than she felt. "No sign of any vehicles around." As they walked up to the house, she could hear the comforting rumble of the ocean. Everything about this scene felt so familiar—and yet it wasn't. Despite spending most of her childhood and adolescence here, she had been down only a few times over the past ten years. "I'm sure everything's just fine here." Why wouldn't it be?

"Well, I want to be sure." Still carrying her bags, he accompanied her up the path of old bricks. She'd helped Dad put these bricks into place when she was twelve. "I don't really like the idea of leaving you out here by yourself without a car, Megan."

"Dad has good neighbors." She pointed north. "I can probably get Mrs. Martin to give me a ride into town in the morning. Then I'll get my tires replaced." As they came up to the little house, she felt a chill run through her. Maybe it was the sea air or the damp fog that she knew was rolling in since she could hear the foghorn blowing over by the jetty. Or maybe it was something else. Like her frazzled nerves.

She had her house key ready. Just like the newspaper office key, she had held on to this one, too. Not so much as a memento, but because her dad always wanted her to feel like she could show up at any time. Even if he was gone on a week-long fishing trip in Mexico. It was similar to a security blanket. A reminder that this was home. Except with Dad gone, she wasn't so sure. Would she be able to feel at home anymore?

"I'll get some lights on." She stepped into the house. "And I need to give you back your jacket, too." As she reached for the entryway light switch, she paused to listen. "Did you hear something?" she whispered to Garret.

He set her bags down in the entryway, holding his forefinger to his lips. They both froze in place, listening intently. But now she heard nothing but the swooshing sound of the waves and the ticking of the clock on the mantel.

"Must've been my imagination," she said quietly as she turned on the entryway light. She looked around the living room, feeling relieved that everything was peacefully in place, from the corny nautical decor that Dad had always loved, to the stone fireplace that probably still smoked on a windy day. She looked wistfully at his worn leather recliner. A new military novel lay on the side table with Dad's reading glasses next to it. Everything was so much the same that she almost expected Dad to come strolling out of the kitchen with a mug of coffee in his hand and a warm grin on his face.

"All's well," she told Garret as she hung her purse on the hall tree next to the still-open front door.

"Seems to be." He looked around in satisfaction. "So I'll bid you good—"

Just then they heard a loud crash from the kitchen.

"Let's get out of here." Garret shoved her toward the door and without questioning him, she exploded out of the house and sprinted back toward his SUV. Garret was right beside her. He opened the passenger-side door for her then ran around to the driver's side. She insisted they get away from here, but Garret didn't start the truck.

"Not yet." He reached beneath the seat to pull out a black hard case then pushed some buttons and removed a revolver.

She felt a jolt of panic. "What's that for?"

"Protection and defense." He looked at the house. "Call the cops and stay put. In fact, stay *down.* Out of sight. And lock the doors." Before she could respond, he was dashing back into the house.

Despite her concerns, she did as he said, hunkering down as she reached around on the floor for her purse and her phone. Then she remembered her purse was hanging on the hall tree by the door, with her phone inside it. She glanced around the darkness of the yard, trying to see what was happening and wishing she'd thought to turn on the porch light.

What if Garret needed help? Despite his instructions to stay put, she quietly opened the door and then, crouching low next to the vehicle, she took in a deep breath. Then she started to sprint toward the house. But halfway there she heard it—the sound of several gunshots in quick sequence.

Had Garret shot someone? Or...? *Please, no, God! Please don't let that be Garret on the wrong side of the gun!*

FIVE

Garret knew it was legal to shoot an intruder during a burglary, but killing this man—no matter what sort of person he might be—was not Garret's goal. But when the intruder jumped him from behind, it was hard to think rationally. The two of them wrestled in the kitchen, tumbled out onto the porch and down the back steps, but when the intruder got away, Garret finally got the chance to take a shot. He aimed below the waist, hoping to get the running man in a leg. But judging by the way the guy kept running, Garret missed.

Garret didn't waste a moment as he took off after him. But in the darkness of the side yard, he lost him in the shadows. Then, as Garret passed by an overgrown hedge, someone jumped him from behind. Once again, they rolled and fought. Garret just about had the guy pinned when he heard the cling of something metallic. Even in the dark, he could see the glint of a switchblade coming toward him.

As he dodged the knife, Garret raised his revolver high, hoping to knock the thug in the head with it, but suddenly someone else jumped into the fray. Garret's revolver was knocked from his hand as he was thrown into the hedge. Just like that, his two assailants disappeared.

Garret scrambled to recover his gun then took off toward the pair who were running toward the road. "Stop or I'll shoot!" he yelled as he sprinted at top speed. He pointed his gun toward them, but knew his chance of hitting either of them in the darkness was slim. Even so, he could not let them escape. Somehow he knew they were connected to Megan's earlier encounter at the newspaper office. And no matter what, he'd get to the bottom of it.

With a pounding heart, Megan ran into the house and grabbed her purse and phone. But the house was silent. Knowing it was risky, she called out for Garret. Hearing no response, and worried the intruder might still be inside, she scurried up the stairs, dialing 911 as she went. She hit Send as she went into her childhood bedroom and locked the door.

As the phone rang, she hurried to the window and peered out into the front yard. Where was Garret? Was he okay? As soon as the dispatcher answered, Megan poured out her whereabouts, their dilemma and her concern over the gunshots. "I need to go to Garret," she told the woman. "He might need me."

The dispatcher continued to insist that Megan remain upstairs, asking more questions about the layout of the house.

"I really should go help Garret." Megan felt a lump in her throat as she imagined him wounded and in need of assistance—or worse.

"Help is on the way. But if there are armed men out there, you should wait for the police to arrive."

"But it's possible Garret is hurt and—"

"They'll be there soon." The dispatcher kept Megan on the line, speaking calmly and soothingly as she asked more questions.

"I'm so worried that Garret needs—"

"Listen! You need to stay where you are until law enforcement arrives," the dispatcher said with authority.

Megan opened the bedroom window, trying to listen for anyone outside. "I hear sirens," she exclaimed.

"It won't be long."

"Can I go downstairs now?" Megan pleaded.

"Wait until the officers give you the all-clear,"

the woman said firmly. "Stay put. Someone will come directly to you. They know where you are."

Megan watched as a small convoy of vehicles with flashing lights pulled in. She could see that at least one was an EMT and wondered if perhaps Garret had called, as well, asking for medical help. Clinging to the windowsill, she prayed silently for his safety. Even though she'd only known him for a few hours—it felt like much more—or perhaps it was simply that she wanted it to be much more. Garret was special. She knew it deep within her. And it wasn't just because he'd been friends with her dad. She knew this was something more—and she couldn't bear to lose him.

As the vehicles parked in front, she could see some of the officers getting out, using their vehicles as a shield, positioning themselves as if to carry out a plan. And then, with firearms drawn and wearing bulletproof vests, several officers cautiously but quickly approached the house.

Megan was almost afraid to breathe as she heard the police entering downstairs. Their footsteps rumbled through the wood floors of the old house and they shouted loudly as doors were opened. And then she heard footsteps on the stairs and someone pounding on her door. "Police!" a female's voice shouted. "Come out with your hands up."

Although she was surprised to be treated like a criminal, Megan knew this was simply routine. And unlocking the door, she held up her hands and stepped out. "I'm Megan McCallister," she said. "I called 911."

"Are you okay?" the uniformed female officer asked, as another officer pushed past them, checking the room to see if anyone else was there.

"Yes." Megan nodded tearfully. "Is Garret okay?"

"I don't know." The officer nodded toward the stairs. "Let's get you out of here and into a cruiser."

Before long, Megan and the female cop were in the backseat of a cruiser, and Megan was answering her questions. As best she could, anyway. Mostly she felt like she was in the dark. "I honestly don't know what happened," she said for the second time. "We heard someone in the house. I'd already been attacked in the newspaper office. So we were sort of on edge. We ran back to the car. Then Garret got out a gun. He went back inside. Shortly after that, I heard the two or three shots."

The questions continued and her nerves ratcheted up until finally, after about half an hour, Megan saw Garret by the front porch. "He's all right!" she shouted. Before the officer could stop her, Megan jumped out of the patrol car and raced toward him.

"You're okay," she exclaimed. "I heard the shots and I was so worried."

He hugged her, holding her longer than was probably necessary, yet she made no move to pull away. "I was worried about you, too," he said tenderly, finally releasing her from the embrace.

"What happened?" She looked into his eyes, feeling that they seemed strangely familiar—as a surprisingly warm rush ran through her.

Garret explained about his wrestling matches with one and then another man. "I chased them for a couple of miles down the beach road."

"So they got away?"

"There was a car with the engine running, waiting for them on Rawlins Road. A dark sedan. Not sure what model or year or anything. Anyway, they got in and took off like a shot. And that was that."

The police came over, asking both of them several more questions and finally allowing them to leave with the promise to remain in touch regarding their whereabouts. Megan could tell that the officers assumed that Garret had simply prevented a burglary, pointing out that it wasn't uncommon for homes to be broken into along this stretch of bluff.

"You don't think this is related to the break-in at the newspaper?" Garret asked.

"Hard to say." The policeman was getting a call on his phone now and, tipping his head, he stepped away.

Garret frowned as he walked her over to his SUV. "Guess we might as well get out of here. Can't imagine you'd want to stay by yourself here tonight."

"Not so much." Megan pondered over what she'd just heard, trying to put the pieces together. "Do you think it was the same guy—the one from the newspaper office?"

"This guy was dressed in dark clothes. Same as the one at the newspaper office. But, like I said, I barely glimpsed that guy's face. But it might've been him. Right height and build and clothes."

"Why is this happening?" she asked with tightly clenched fists. "What is going on? What does all this mean?"

He ran his hand through his damp hair, making it curl even more. "I, uh, I have a theory."

"Really?"

"I told the police about it. Not sure they took me seriously, though."

"I still want to hear it."

He glanced over his shoulder. "How about if I get your bags from the house first?"

"Thanks."

After he loaded her things into the back of the SUV, he explained what was going on with the police inside the house. "Where am I taking you?" he asked as he backed out, maneuvering past the emergency vehicles.

"Oh, yeah, I better call a hotel." She pulled out her phone, doing a quick search for the largest hotel in town. But to her dismay, the desk clerk informed her they had no vacancies. "Really?" Megan asked. "You have nothing?"

"It's Memorial Day weekend," the clerk said in a tired voice. "And the weather's pretty nice. From what I hear everyone is full up in town."

"Oh." Megan thanked her, hung up and then told Garret.

"Yeah, I was worried about that, too," he said. "Even my cabins are full. And I had to turn folks away. But I do have a couple of vacant cabins that I'm still working on. I didn't book them out because I haven't had time to finish them yet. You could sort of camp there for the night…if you don't mind roughing it some."

"Oh…" Megan imagined a dirty old fishing cabin with a lumpy mattress, but was so tired she didn't even care.

"Come to think of it, Cabin A is nearly finished."

She looked at the clock, surprised to see that it

was well after midnight now. "I'm so exhausted, I don't care if the place is a mess, Garret. As long as it's safe." She looked over at him. "Do you think it's safe there? At the marina?"

"Don't know why it wouldn't be."

She sighed. "Yeah, but I don't know why my dad's house wasn't safe, either."

"Good point." He shook his head. "But I'm sure you'll be safe at the marina. The cabin you'll have is right next to mine and I'm a pretty light sleeper. Not only that, but I'll let you have Rocky, too."

"Rocky?"

"My Doberman."

"A guard dog?"

"Well, he *looks* like a guard dog and acts like a guard dog. But he's actually quite harmless. More of an alarm than an attack dog." He glanced at her. "Do you like dogs?"

"Absolutely. And if you honestly don't mind sharing him, I'd love to have Rocky stay with me tonight. That would be reassuring."

"Great."

As Garret drove them toward town, Megan tried to wrap her head around all that had happened since arriving at Cape Perpetua just a few hours ago. It was mind-boggling, and frightening and unreal.

Instead of taking the river road directly to the

marina, Garret turned into town. "I'm doing a little detour," he explained. "Just in case anyone wanted to follow us. Although I haven't really noticed any suspicious cars."

She looked all around, relieved to see that the town was pretty deserted. She didn't see a single set of headlights anywhere. Garret seemed satisfied, too, and, taking a backstreet and a couple more turns, they were soon at the marina.

"Here we are," Garret announced as he parked next to the boxy building that housed the old store where she and Dad used to buy treats for their fishing trips. "Welcome to Larsson's Marina." He cautiously looked all around as he helped her out. "I'll get your bags."

Before long, he was opening the door of one of the small cabins alongside the river. "Like I said, it's still a little rough." He set her bags inside the door. "I'll grab you some bedding and towels and stuff. But I think you'll be okay for one night."

She nodded as she looked around the small space. "This will be fine," she assured him. "I really appreciate it."

"I'll be right back."

After he left she examined the cabin more carefully. With new pine floors and pine-paneled walls, the room smelled clean and fresh. The mattress on the queen-size bed was brand-new, too, still wrapped in factory plastic. The tiny bathroom, although missing a door and a coat of paint, had new fixtures, including a large mirror. But she didn't recognize the stranger looking back at her. The pale skin, strained features, dark circles beneath her hazel eyes and that messy long hair—who was that poor woman, anyway? Megan simply turned away.

As she unzipped one of her bags, she noticed that the narrow closet, also missing its door, had no rod or hangers. Well, Garret hadn't promised it'd be the Ritz. She was just removing a T-shirt to sleep in when a knock on the front door made her jump.

"It's just me," Garret said quietly.

She unlocked the door, opening it to let him enter. His arms were full of bedding and towels, and behind him came a big sleek brown dog, eager to sniff her.

"You must be Rocky," she said, allowing him to smell the back of her hand. "My new roommate."

"Yeah, I invited Rocky to come check you out." Garret dumped the pile onto the mattress. "If you guys like each other, I'll go get his bed."

She knelt down to scratch him behind the ears, and his tail wagged happily. "You're a good boy, aren't you?" She already felt safer, just having him here.

"Sorry I don't have a curtain up yet." Garret pointed to the bare window. "But I brought some extra towels." He handed her a couple of white towels. "Just hang them over the rod for now."

"Thanks." She went over to hang and adjust her terry curtains. Rocky followed her, watching with canine interest.

"I'll be right back with Rocky's bed."

She put some things away and soon Garret returned with a big dog bed, shoving it into the corner by the door. "Sorry not to have the place in better shape, but—"

"I think this is a lovely little cabin," she assured him. "And I'm happy to make myself at home. Thank you."

He grinned. "Before I go, how about if we exchange phone numbers? Just in case." He pulled out a business card, handing it to her. Then she went to her purse and did the same.

"Thanks, Garret," she said in a tired voice. "For everything."

"Sleep well," he told her. "Remember I'm next door." He pointed to his right.

She thanked him again and after he left, bolted the door. Then, just to be sure, she checked the window, making certain it was locked, as well. Finally, although she felt certain it would be a sleepless night, she started to make her bed. Rocky watched for a while as she peeled off the plastic and put on the sheets, but he soon grew bored and decided to make himself comfortable on his own bed.

It was after one by the time she finally got settled and pulled on her T-shirt and flannel pants then tumbled into bed. Despite her concerns about sleeping, she realized she was too exhausted to fight it.

Megan woke with a start to a loud, unfamiliar sound. A dog barking? Where was she? She stumbled out of bed, remembering that she was in Cape Perpetua, in the marina cabin—and the dog belonged to Garret. "Rocky," she said urgently. "What is it?"

The dog continued to bark aggressively. In the semi-darkness she could see Rocky's shadowy silhouette in front of the door—he was definitely on high alert about something outside.

"What's out there?" she whispered as she cowered behind him. She didn't want to discourage him from barking—especially if there was someone dangerous outside her door. But she also remembered what Garret had said. He was a better alarm than protector. She hurried back to the bed, feeling all over for where she'd left her purse and phone. Why wasn't it here? Suddenly, she heard a pounding on the wooden door, which made Rocky bark even louder. Megan's heart raced as she got down on the wooden floor, grasping all around for her purse and phone. Where was it? And who was at the door? And would this madness ever end?

SIX

"Megan?" Garret yelled to be heard over Rocky's loud, incessant barking—the same barking that had woken him just minutes earlier. "Are you okay?" When she didn't answer, he started to pound harder on her door, wishing he'd thought to grab his set of master keys. "Megan!" he yelled again, this time at the top of his lungs. "Are you okay?"

"Garret?" she cried.

"Yes, it's me," he confirmed. "Open the door."

The door cracked open and Megan stuck her head out just as Garret commanded Rocky to be quiet. Fortunately, the dog obeyed. "What's going on?" he asked Megan.

"I don't know," she answered in a shaky voice. "I was sound asleep and then he started to bark."

Garret looked over his shoulder toward the marina, where the dark sky was just turning gray along the eastern horizon. "He must've heard something out here. But you're okay?"

She nodded with a troubled expression.

He looked out over the river now, seeing there was a slight wake rocking the marina's dock. Since it was nearly five, it wasn't too early for a crabbing or fishing boat to be heading out to sea. Unless it was something else.

"Go back to bed," he told her. "I'll go sniff around."

"Do you want to take Rocky with you?" she offered. "For help?"

He forced a smile. "No. You better keep him here with you. And make sure you lock the door." He waited as she closed and locked it then headed over to the dock to investigate. He scanned up and down the river, but didn't see any running lights, something a legitimate fishing boat would use before sunrise, but there was definitely a wake from a boat passing by. He peered out over the water, just starting to reflect light from the predawn sky. And suddenly, he saw it, the dark outline of a boat—probably a thirty-footer—heading out toward the ocean. But with no lights.

Garret was tempted to hop in his Kingfisher and take off after them. The twenty-footer had an outboard engine that could catch most anything out there. But then what? Inform the boaters that their running lights weren't on? And what if they really were criminals and it turned dangerous? Was he ready for that?

He'd heard enough stories from the coast guard, as well as his grandpa—mostly about illegal fishing and occasionally drug running—and he knew it could get dicey fast out on the water.

As Garret walked past the marina, he noticed that the sliding door to the mechanic shop was partly open. And he knew that he'd locked it yesterday morning, after moving Rory's Jeep into it for safe-keeping.

Through his thick flannel shirt, Garret touched the holster that he'd strapped around his waist as he dashed out to check on Megan and Rocky. His grandpa had taught him to use and respect firearms as a youth, explaining that running a marina in a rural Oregon coastal town could sometimes get rough. He needed to be prepared.

Thankfully, Garret had never had to use a gun at the marina. In fact, the incident at Rory's house last night was the first time he'd ever shot a firearm at a human. And it was not something he cared to do again. Despite what some of the gun experts said—like "shoot to kill"—Garret preferred the idea of shooting to *stop* someone. A way to bring them to justice. Especially someone dangerous, like the thug who had nearly killed Megan last night. He'd love to put that guy behind bars.

Was it possible that same thug was here at the marina now? And if so, why? And how had he figured out that Megan was here? Or was this even related to Megan? Perhaps she had simply been in the wrong place at the wrong time. Garret slowly crept up to the shop, trying to put together a plan and, at the same time, trying to figure this puzzle out.

He suspected that the guy in the black pants and sweatshirt at the newspaper office hadn't planned on knocking off Megan. He'd probably been after something else—something that Rory had left behind. And Megan had simply gotten in his way. That was Garret's theory. Something he'd tried to share with Michael earlier, but it had sounded so far-fetched that Garret even had a problem believing it. Maybe when the coroner finished his autopsy on Rory's body they would know more.

With his revolver in his right hand, Garret patted the chest pocket of his flannel shirt with his left hand, making sure his phone was still there. Then he pressed his back against the side of the shop, attempting to peek inside the cracked door. It was too dark inside to see a thing, but he could see that the lock had been forced. Someone had definitely broken in. Probably what Rocky had been barking about.

Garret's heart was pounding hard as he reached

inside the opening, feeling the interior wall for the light switch that he knew was next to the door. His plan was to turn it on, slide open the door and jump inside—all at the same time. The surprise effect.

Taking in a deep breath, he did it, leaping into the shop just as the overhead fluorescent lights flickered on. With his gun drawn and ready, he braced himself for whatever came next. But he saw and heard no one. Still, he ducked behind a cabin cruiser that was in for repairs. Hunkered down by the trailer wheels, he just listened. Still nothing.

Knowing someone had been there, was maybe still in there, he decided to work his way around the perimeter of the shop—no small task since there were tools and cans and all sorts of nautical stuff strewn about. Note to self, he thought ironically, tell his newest and not most reliable employee to clean this place up. If Kent was even coming back.

By the time he'd crept around the perimeter of the shop, he felt certain that whoever had broken in was gone. Probably on that stealth boat that he'd spotted heading out to sea. He went over to where he'd parked Rory's dark green Jeep Wrangler yesterday. Just seeing the vehicle sent a wave of sadness through him. Megan was right. Rory had been too young to die. He'd been in great health and had been looking forward to decades more of fishing. Such a shame.

Garret ran his hand over the cloth roof of the Jeep but stopped when he reached what felt like a slit on the driver's side. He looked more closely and, sure enough, someone had cut through the roof. And the door on the driver's side was unlocked. Someone had gotten into Rory's Jeep.

Garret opened the driver's-side door, looking inside. The compartments were both opened and their contents were strewn around. Someone had obviously been looking for something.

"Hello?"

Garret jumped, hitting his head on the roofline bar. He recognized her voice and felt embarrassed for being so jumpy. "Megan?" he called back, rubbing his head.

"Is everything okay? We were getting worried."

Rocky came bounding over to him, and Garret leaned down to stroke his smooth coat. "Hey, there, buddy. Did you keep Megan safe?"

"He was an excellent guard," Megan said as she joined him. She frowned at the Jeep. "Is this my dad's?"

"Yeah." He pointed to the slit in the roof. "Someone broke into my shop...and they broke into Rory's Jeep, too." He pulled out his phone. "I was just about to call someone about it."

"911 again?"

"Nah, I'll just call Michael this time. Put it on his radar."

As he explained to the lieutenant about the break-in, Megan bent down to look inside the Jeep. She gathered up the scattered papers, stacking the vehicle manual, insurance information and registration together. With a deep sigh, she held them to her chest and then, almost reverently, she slid them back into the glove compartment. Garret knew she was in pain over the loss of her dad, but it would be hard for her to deal with her grief if this madness continued. He knew she was strong, but he wondered how much she could take.

He finished his conversation with Michael, slipping his phone back into his pocket, just as Megan stood up from straightening the Jeep. She looked at him with an uneasy expression. "I just don't understand it, Garret. Something is going on here. But what is it? And why?"

"I have some ideas." Garret glanced at his watch. "Maybe we can discuss it over breakfast. I'm starved. How about you?"

She nodded. "I'm hungry, too."

"Well, I've been told I make a pretty mean omelet," he said as he led her out of the shop, sliding the door closed. "Care to give it a try?"

"Sounds good to me."

As they walked over to his cabin, he noticed that she'd changed into jeans, a plaid shirt and a sturdy-looking pair of walking boots. She looked much less like a city girl now. More suited to Cape Perpetua. And she looked pretty, too. She looked like the kind of girl he'd dreamed of meeting someday. Although he'd dreamed of different circumstances.

"Welcome," he said as he opened the door to the largest cabin, the one that had belonged to his grandparents.

"Wow, this is nice," she said as she went inside.

"Thanks. My grandma had some renovations made, back in the nineties. There are some things I'd still like to change, but I've been focusing my efforts—and budget—on the fishing cabins, instead."

"For fishing cabins, they seem pretty nice." She went over to the big picture window that faced the river. "Wow, what a view."

"Yeah, I like it. Feel free to look around while I start on breakfast."

She went to the oversize fireplace. "I love these river stones." She ran her hand over the wood mantel, without mentioning the dust he knew was there. His housekeeping skills weren't the greatest.

"Let's see." He opened the fridge, looking to

see what kind of options he might have to fill an omelet. "I've got mushrooms and spinach and onions and cheese and—"

"Those all sound good," she said with enthusiasm.

"Okay." He started setting the ingredients out on the counter by the stove.

"Need any help?"

"Do you like coffee?"

"Love it."

"Know how to make it?"

"I think I can figure it out," she said with a trace of sarcasm as she went over to where the coffeemaker was next to the sink, making herself busy.

As he chopped the veggies and shredded cheese, he felt grateful to his grandmother for insisting that he learn to cook as a teenager. He didn't like to brag—especially to his macho friends—but he was pretty comfortable in the kitchen.

With the coffee brewing, Megan came over to watch him. "Looks like you know what you're doing," she observed. "Impressive."

As he started to cook the omelet she sat down at the breakfast bar. "I have so many questions, Garret. Even more now than I had last night. I almost don't know where to begin."

"I know." He flipped the jumbo-size omelet

then slipped a couple pieces of rye bread into the toaster. "I probably have a lot of the same questions."

"And it's hard to process losing my dad," she continued. "I mean, with all these questions racing through my head. And at the same time, I feel like I should watch my back. Like I'm not safe. You know?"

"I know." He got out a pair of mugs, filling them with coffee. "Take anything in yours?" He held a steaming mug out to her.

"Just black."

He set it in front of her. "I can't guarantee your safety, Megan. But I think this place is as safe as anywhere. For right now, anyway."

"Then you're worried?"

He nodded grimly as he buttered their toast. "Yeah."

"Do you have any idea about what's going on?"

With his back to her, he slid the omelet onto the plate, divided it into two halves then set a piece of buttered toast next to them. "Voila," he said as he held out the plates. "Why don't we take them outside. It's pretty mild out there."

She picked up their coffees and followed him out to the terrace that overlooked the river. It was flooded with morning sunshine.

"This is wonderful out here," she said as she

sat down at the small dining table. "It almost makes me happy."

He sighed as he sat down across from her. "I know…it's hard to be happy in light of everything, Megan. But things will get better."

She looked out over the water. "I hope so."

"Do you mind if I say a blessing?"

She looked surprised, but simply nodded. "Not at all."

And so, feeling a little self-conscious, he bowed his head and prayed. Not only for the food, but for their safety, as well. "Amen."

"Amen," she echoed. "Thanks."

For a minute or so neither of them spoke, just quietly ate. After a while, Garret made small talk, but eventually, when they were both done, he brought up the subject they were both eager to discuss. "I think something is going on here, Megan," he confessed. "I thought so when Rory's boat went down. But everyone kept saying I was imagining things. Detective Greene even suggested I was nurturing a conspiracy theory."

"Who's Detective Greene?"

"Detective Greene is Cape Perpetua PD's first official detective. The city hired him shortly after several corrupt policemen were removed from the department—just a few months ago."

"Oh, yeah. Dad told me about those cops

who were involved in human trafficking. That was horrible."

"Pretty shocking for a small town like ours." He frowned as he remembered the scandal. "So I guess I'm not too surprised…"

"Surprised by what?"

He wondered how much he should disclose to her. And yet he felt she had the right to know everything—or at least as much as he knew—although he hated to overwhelm her. She'd already been through so much. "That there are still some crime elements around."

"So this Detective Greene… Is he okay? On the up and up?" She studied him closely.

"I don't distrust him personally but he's not what I'd call very experienced."

"I see." Her brow creased in frustration as she ran her hand over her wavy auburn hair as if trying to tame it, although he didn't see the need. "And what about your conspiracy theory?"

"Well, I just wasn't buying that Rory had a heart attack out there."

She nodded eagerly. "Yes! That's exactly how I feel."

"I felt like something was wrong with that story, but the police and coast guard seemed to accept it at face value. And then, after you were attacked in the newspaper office—and the intruder at your dad's house—I knew it wasn't a coincidence. And now someone broke into his Jeep." He scratched his head. "Although I'd like to know how anyone knew that I'd put it in there. Anyway, it all seems to point to some serious foul play—and it's starting to add up."

"I agree. But what does it add up to? What is going on here?"

He sighed. "I was reluctant to tell you, Megan. Worried that just knowing about it—I mean my, uh, theory—that it might put you in danger."

"I'm already in danger," she pointed out.

"Yeah. Exactly." He took a sip of coffee.

"Here's my guess." She leaned forward with an intent look in her dark brown eyes. "Dad was investigating something illegal. He planned to print it in the newspaper. And his exposé would get someone into some serious trouble."

Garret simply nodded.

"Somehow the criminals found out. And they wanted to shut him up. But that wasn't enough. They wanted to find whatever it was he'd been working on, too. So they could dispose of it. And that's why they broke into the office. And his house. And probably his Jeep, too."

Garret stared in amazement. "Impressive. You must be a really good investigative journalist."

"Thanks." But she looked dismayed. "I was actually hoping I was wrong."

"Well, you could be wrong." He set down his

mug, gazing out over the river as a couple of crabbing boats headed toward the ocean, questioning just how much he should tell her. The more she knew, the more dangerous it would become for her. So far, she might've just been in the wrong place at the wrong time. If she went home to Seattle, she'd probably never hear another word about this. She'd be safe.

Her question interrupted his thoughts. "But you don't think so, do you?"

He pursed his lips, trying to think of the best plan...the safest plan...for her.

"You know something, Garret. I can tell you do. I could tell last night." She set her coffee cup down with a clunk. "Tell me what you think is going on. I have a right to know."

"Maybe. But what if it puts you in harm's way?"

"Like I'm not?" she shot back. "A creep nearly slit my throat last night."

"Yes. But that's only because you got in his way. He wasn't going after you personally, Megan."

"I'm not so sure about that." She pursed her lips. "That guy paused in the middle of everything to text someone. Don't you think that's weird?"

Garret shrugged, even though he agreed with her. It did seem weird.

"And then it was like he waited, like he was getting his instructions from someone else. And it honestly felt like he'd been instructed to kill me."

Garret still felt uncertain. Wouldn't it be safer for her to remain somewhat oblivious? Not that he could keep her in the dark when she'd already started to figure things out. She was a smart girl.

"Tell me what's going on," she demanded. "This is about *my* dad. I deserve to know."

"I understand your curiosity. But I'm not convinced it's in your best interest, Megan. Sometimes ignorance is more than just bliss. Sometimes it can save your life."

"It wouldn't have last night."

He knew she was right. He studied her for a long moment, trying not to get too pulled in by her good looks. Just because she was extremely attractive didn't mean she should get her way. However, he knew she was more than just a pretty face. She was intelligent and caring—and he didn't want to see her hurt.

"I know you think you're protecting me." She spoke solemnly, gazing out over the river with a faraway look. "But I'm a lot tougher than I look. I can take it."

He closed his eyes, trying to figure out how her dad would have him handle this. Wouldn't Rory want Garret to watch out for his only daughter? Wouldn't he want to keep her safe? Keep her alive?

"Garret." Megan grabbed him by the arm. "Get down!"

"What—?" Before he opened his eyes, she jerked him down to the deck, where she was already on her knees and hunkered down low. In the same instant, he heard a gunshot and the sliding glass door behind them exploded, shattering into thousands of tiny pieces.

SEVEN

"Where'd that shot come from?" Garret asked as they remained hunkered beneath the table.

"A fishing boat," she whispered, although she knew the shooter couldn't possibly hear them. She glanced uneasily at the shrubbery beside the deck's railing, the only thing shielding them from the river where the shot had originated.

"Let's get inside." He reached for her hand, nudging her in ahead of him. "Careful of the glass. And stay low."

As they made their way through the shattered door, Megan heard the sound of a boat engine revving up behind them. "Do you think they're leaving?" she asked in a shaky voice.

"Sounds like it." Garret already had his phone out and by the time they were in the living room, she could hear the 911 dispatcher on the other end. Garret quickly explained what had just transpired, assuring the dispatcher that no one had been shot. "Contact the coast guard," he instructed, giving the location. "Let me see if I can find out." He looked at Megan. "Did you see what kind of boat it was?"

She nodded, and Garret put the phone on speaker.

"It looked like a regular fishing boat," she said, trying to remember details about the rather nondescript vessel. "I think it had a metal hull. Dark color, like black or navy. Maybe charcoal. And it was outfitted with poles, like they were heading out to fish. It was probably about twenty feet, with a covered cabin. I think a soft top. It wasn't white, though. Kind of matched the boat."

"How many on the boat?" the dispatcher asked.

"I'd guess at least two because someone had to be at the helm. Plus the guy in the back with the gun."

"And what happened exactly? Before the gunshot."

Megan tried to think. "Well, we were sitting outside. I'd been looking over the river and I noticed a boat moving along, heading west toward the ocean. But it was fairly close to the north shore, you know, where the marina is located. It just seemed like a regular fishing boat, except they were sort of meandering. Like they weren't in a hurry to get on the ocean. Then I noticed the boat really slowed down right before the marina. I wondered if maybe they planned to stop for something. Then suddenly a guy in the back of the boat stood up with what looked like a long gun. I think it had a scope because it looked sort of bulky, you know? And then he pointed it right at us. That's when I said *get down*."

"Do you know what kind of long gun? Automatic? Semiautomatic? Shotgun?"

"I really don't know. But like I said, it looked kind of bulky. Not like my dad's hunting rifles, you know?"

"Judging by the window," Garret injected, "and the distance down to the river, I'd guess it was a high-powered rifle. Can't say if it was automatic or not, since only one shot was fired. But I think I can see where the bullet went inside the house." He pointed over to the dining room table. Megan looked over to see a spot that looked splintered.

"Don't touch anything," the dispatcher said. "Wait for police to get there."

"Did you contact the coast guard yet?" he asked eagerly. "That boat's probably crossing the bar by now."

"The coast guard is notified."

As Garret continued talking to the dispatcher, Megan stepped away. Her legs were still shaking and her stomach felt like it was tied in a knot as she sat down on the couch. Why was this happening? She was on the verge of tears again, but then Rocky came over, laying his head in her lap as if to comfort her. As she rubbed his silky ears, she began to relax a little. "I'm glad you didn't get hurt," she said softly.

She could hear Garret assuring the dispatcher that they were in no immediate danger, but he sounded eager to get off the phone. Finally, as the sound of sirens grew nearer, he convinced the dispatcher that he needed to hang up.

"I sure hope the coast guard picks them up," he told Megan as he went to the front of the house, looking out the front window toward the marina. "I need to go let Wade in."

"Wade?"

"He works for me." Garret waved outside. "If you don't mind being alone for a couple minutes, I'll go tell him what's up and let him into the store."

"I'll be fine." She patted Rocky's back. "I've got my protector here."

Garret opened the door, cautiously looking to the right and left.

"You be careful," she called out.

"You, too."

After Garret left, she could hear the sirens getting closer. Surely the police should be growing quite concerned by now. This was their third response since she'd arrived in Cape Perpetua yesterday. Maybe Michael would rethink his assumption that her dad had died of natural causes out on the ocean.

Several minutes passed before Garret returned with a young man in plain clothes as well as a couple of uniformed officers. Rocky, true to form, began barking uncontrollably, using his bark and imposing stance to keep the policemen at the door.

"Let me put him in the laundry room." Garret hurried over to get Rocky, leading him out through the kitchen.

"I'm Detective Greene." A young man in plain clothes introduced himself to Megan, shaking her hand as he glanced around the room. He was just introducing her to the other two officers when Garret returned. And then Garret took them all over to see where the bullet had shattered the sliding door.

Megan went over to the front window, sitting down on the couch where she could look outside. Another pair of policemen was strolling about the marina, looking around the docks and cabins and shop area. She felt relieved to have them around, but at the same time she felt rattled. She also questioned what good it did for these policemen to go poking around the marina when the shooter had clearly taken off toward the ocean. But hopefully the coast guard boys were out there chasing them down. She felt she'd gotten a pretty good description of the boat.

After a few minutes of looking both inside and outside, the youthful detective came back to speak to Megan, sitting across from her on the arm of an overstuffed chair. "I heard about your encounter at the newspaper office last night," he began. "Lieutenant Conrad shared his report. That must've been frightening for you."

"I'm just glad to know someone is investigating all this." She studied him, trying to guess his age. He looked like he was barely out of high school.

"I would've started on the case last night," he explained. "But I was attending an out-of-town conference. Headed back as soon as I heard what was going on here. Mind if I ask you some questions?"

"Not at all."

Garret came back into the living room, excusing himself to take care of some marina business outside. "Make yourselves at home," he told everyone. "Just ring that brass ship's bell on the front porch if you need me and I'll come running." He grinned at Megan. "My grandma trained me to answer to that bell."

"Thanks," Detective Greene told him. "I'll have more questions for you later."

"I have some questions for you, too." Garret grabbed a ball cap as he opened the door.

Despite her concern over the detective's youth, Megan was more than eager to cooperate with him. But she soon found herself getting frustrated. Unless she was imagining things, this guy seemed much less concerned by the recent crime spree than she was. Of course, she told herself, he was probably just being reserved and professional. As a journalist, she'd witnessed law enforcement's nonchalance before. And it wasn't as if he wasn't listening to her. He did appear to be taking careful notes on his iPad.

"So...don't you think these incidents must be related?" she finally asked him. "And in that case, doesn't it seem unlikely that my dad's death resulted from natural causes? Or was even accidental?"

"I'm waiting for the coroner's report."

"I respect that. But don't you think that time is of the essence?"

"Time is always of the essence." His tone sounded slightly defensive, which she found aggravating.

"Aren't you curious as to why someone would break into my dad's office last night, the day after his death? And then someone breaks into his house, as well? Isn't that more than just a coincidence?" she demanded.

"That's what I plan to find out."

"And his Jeep, too," she added. "What are these people looking for, anyway?"

"What's this about his Jeep?" Detective Greene looked up from his iPad.

"My dad's Jeep was broken into, as well. Garret just discovered it early this morning. He called Lieutenant Conrad about it." She explained about their predawn awakening. "Rocky heard someone out there. And when Garret went out to investigate, he felt certain the intruder had just been there."

"No one told me about that."

"From what I can see, that's four crimes. Five counting my dad's death. This is a big case, Detective. I hope you're taking it seriously."

"Of course I'm taking it seriously." He frowned. "Are you questioning me?"

She tried not to take offense at what seemed a rude reaction. "Well, I have to admit you seem rather young to be a detective."

He sat up straighter. "I have a masters in forensic science from a highly reputable university. Graduated top of my class. Be assured, Miss McCallister, I know what I'm doing."

"Good," she said nervously. "Glad to hear it. The truth is I'm feeling pretty scared right now. I grew up in Cape Perpetua. I'm not used to feeling unsafe in this town. I mean, it was never like this before."

"Well, things change. I've only been here a few months, but from what I hear, Cape Perpetua is evolving into a real tourist town. It's not unusual for crime to follow growth." He stood up. "And since this is Memorial Day weekend, the town is busier than usual. It's not surprising that there are some rowdies acting up. We've already had twice as many calls this year than the previous Memorial Day weekend. And it's only Saturday."

Megan felt indignant, wanting to point out that most of those calls had probably been related to her dad and herself. "Certainly, you're not suggesting these recent incidents are the result of tourists behaving badly?"

"I'm sorry to say that discharging firearms from fishing boats, although illegal, isn't highly unusual on a holiday weekend in a small fishing town. Just ask the coast guard."

"Yes, but—"

"If you'll excuse me, Miss McCallister, I'd like to question Mr. Larsson now."

She nodded. "Don't let me keep you."

As he left, she felt irritated. She didn't know what she'd expected him to do—or how to react. But his casual attitude about this case was truly aggravating. As she stood up, she suspected that she'd offended him by questioning his age and inexperience. But she'd only wanted some re-assurance—some encouragement that he was taking this thing seriously. Was that too much to ask?

She went over to the front window, watching as Detective Greene waved to Garret. Several uniformed officers were still out there, but mostly they seemed to be standing around, admiring the boats. Why weren't they looking for something? Or someone? Was no one taking this seriously?

At the same time she knew that there probably wasn't much to investigate out there. The shooting had occurred from the river. It wasn't like that boat had left any kind of tracks. But what about the break-in of the mechanics shop? And Dad's Jeep?

"Looks like we're done in here," a policeman told her as they prepared to leave the house.

"Did you find the bullet?" she asked.

The shorter cop held up a plastic bag with some wood shards and a piece of metal that she assumed was a bullet.

"Wow, that looks lethal," she said.

He just nodded.

As they left, Megan felt even more uneasy. She knew enough about law enforcement to know that cops liked to keep their information to themselves. And, in their defense, it was procedural. Usually to protect an investigation. Being a journalist had taught her that much. She also knew that cops didn't like being questioned. It was their job to question others. She just hoped she hadn't burned her bridge with Detective Greene. Nevertheless she suspected he was fresh out of college, with little experience on the ground. It made sense that he'd taken a job in a small town like Cape Perpetua. Probably hoping to cut his teeth before moving on. Just the same, his cavalier attitude was unacceptable. Her dad deserved better!

Seeing no reason to remain in Garret's house, she decided to return to her cabin to pack her things. It had been generous of Garret to allow her to stay in what was clearly an unfinished space, but she didn't want to wear out her welcome.

Still, as she packed her bags, she was unsure as to where she would go next. The hotels were full until Monday. And her dad's house—after last night—didn't feel safe. Besides that, she wondered, as she zipped her bag closed, how was she going to get there with four flat tires?

She got out her phone, calling AAA to see about getting her tires fixed. To her relief, they offered to take care of the car, but she would need to meet them there to hand off her keys.

Remembering Dad's Jeep, she wondered if he still kept a spare key in the little magnetic box on the left side of the engine. It was a practice he'd started long ago, after losing his keys while fishing.

She set her bags next to the cabin door then proceeded over to the mechanic's shop, sliding the big metal door open to let herself inside. As she walked over to her dad's Jeep she wondered how Garret had gotten it into the shop. Maybe he knew about the key. Perhaps he had it now. But she opened the hood and there, sure enough, was the dusty old magnet box with the key still inside.

She slid the big door open wide enough to back out and before long she was parked in front of the little cabin, loading her things into the small backseat.

"What're you doing?" Detective Greene demanded as she closed the passenger-side door.

"What?" She peered curiously at him.

"You're tampering with evidence."

"But it's my dad's Jeep," she told him.

"We haven't gathered prints yet."

"Oh." She bit her lower lip, realizing she should've known better. Maybe he was doing his job, after all. "I'm sorry." She reached inside and turned off the ignition and removed the key.

"You do want us to do our job, don't you?" He narrowed his eyes slightly.

"Well, I figured you'd had plenty of time to go over the Jeep by now," she shot back. "It's been more than an hour." She glanced to where a couple of cops were standing on the dock, admiring a sailboat that was for sale.

"Well, we haven't." He waved to the officers, calling them over.

Feeling the need to bite her tongue, Megan walked away from the Jeep. Standing off to the side of the cabin she crossed her arms in front of her, not bothering to hide her irritation.

"Hey." Garret joined her. "How'd you get the Jeep out of the shop?"

She held up the key. "Dad's backup key."

He rolled his eyes. "Wish I'd known about that before I pushed it into the shop yesterday." He flexed a muscle. "Good workout, though."

She frowned over to where the cops were now converged all around her dad's Jeep, acting like it contained all the clues to their case. "I just got chewed out for tampering with evidence," she said quietly.

"Oh?"

"Yeah. I figured they'd had enough time to look through it." She shoved the key into her jeans pocket. "And I didn't even confess that I'd already handled some of the paperwork when

I put it back in the glove box." She shrugged. "Guess I'll see if they can figure that one out." She turned to Garret. "Do you think that detective knows what he's doing? He seems awfully young to me."

"He is young." Garret sighed. "And new to Cape Perpetua. First time we've had a real detective. But there had been some crimes recently— reason for the police department to make room in the budget for a detective."

"And Detective Greene was all they could afford," she offered.

He nodded. "Your dad didn't have much confidence in him, either. Called him Detective Greenhorn."

She grimaced. "That sounds like Dad."

Garret reached for her arm, pulling her over to the space between the cabins as if to keep his next words confidential. "Rory had been working on a story, Megan," he said with a quiet intensity. "He'd been doing some investigative journalism. And the young detective had not been very helpful."

"Do you think Greene was being intentionally difficult?" she asked in a hushed tone. "Trying to cover for someone?"

"I doubt that. I think he's just inexperienced and doesn't like anyone knowing more than he does."

She nodded. "That's kind of how I felt, too."

Garret's brows arched. "Did you rub him wrong, too?"

"Probably." She gave him a sheepish smile. "And I'm not even sure I care."

Garret smiled. "You're your father's daughter."

"Thank you." She told Garret a story about Dad getting in hot water with the police over his "investigative reporting" back when she was a teen. "I always felt proud of Dad for standing up to them, though. In my mind, he was the quintessential newspaper man. I wanted to grow up to be just like him."

Garret told her a tale of his own about Rory—a fishing story involving a shark and a half-eaten halibut—and it was so hilarious that they were both laughing so hard they actually got tears in their eyes. But it felt therapeutic to her. She knew that her dad's life was something that should be celebrated. He wouldn't want her to be upset and depressed. He'd always despised gloomy funerals, claiming that he wanted his friends to gather and remember him, not mourn him. She still needed to make arrangements for a memorial service. As well as a lot of other things.

"I have so much to do." She pointed over to where the cops seemed to be finishing up with the Jeep. "Do you think they're done yet?"

"Let's find out." He led her over to them.

"I really need to get to town," she said quietly.

"If you could wait about an hour, I could take you in," he offered.

"A tow truck is on its way to my car right now. They might even be there already. I promised to meet them, to give them a key."

Garret went over to Detective Greene, explaining the situation and after ascertaining that they were done, he opened the driver's door for Megan. As she got in, he pointed to her luggage in the backseat. "Does this mean you're checking out?"

"Oh, yeah." She felt embarrassed. "I forgot to pay you, but I can—"

"No, no, that's not it. I'm just curious as to where you'll be staying. Town's pretty booked up, you know."

"I know." She frowned. "Maybe Dad's place—"

"No," he said quickly. "I don't think that's wise."

She nodded. "You're probably right."

"But I can understand you wanting something more luxurious than what I have to offer."

"No, I love your little cabin. But I realize it's not ready for occupancy yet. I hate being in the way if you're trying to get it finished—"

"Don't worry about that." He closed the Jeep door, leaning down to look in her eyes. "You're very welcome here, Megan. I mean that. And I'd feel better knowing you're close by. I think your dad would agree, too. Besides, Rocky is going to miss you if you leave." He smiled. "I'll miss you too."

She felt another warm rush run through her. "Okay," she said a bit breathlessly. "When I get done with everything in town—and that might take a while—I'll be back."

He pointed to her bags again. "Might as well leave those here."

So she got out and together they extracted her bags. "Thanks, Garret." She watched as he gathered her luggage. "I don't know what I'd have done without your help so far." She really didn't want to leave him now. Not just because he made her feel safe either. But she had business to attend to, and so she just thanked him and started the engine.

He made a concerned frown. "Just be careful out there, Megan. Watch your back."

"I will." But as she pulled out of the marina, she felt uncertain and unsettled. If someone was out there with a high-powered rifle, how was it possible to watch her back? For all she knew, the gunman from the boat could be lurking behind one of the many evergreen trees along the river right now. Or positioned along the road, waiting for her to drive into town, with his long dark gun ready, its scope pointing directly at her head.

Once again, prayer seemed her only defense. So with one eye on the road, and one eye watching the shadows alongside it, she prayed all the way back into town.

EIGHT

She was barely out of sight when Garret felt uneasy. Why had he let her leave like that? All by herself in the soft-topped Jeep that offered zero protection against a crazed gunman. It went against everything inside him. And yet the police, especially Detective Greene, were all acting so laid-back. It was as if their indifference had become contagious. But he should know better. He set her bags inside Cabin A, relieved to know that at least she'd be back here for the night. And she could have Rocky with her again.

Even so, as he went back outside, he was tempted to jump in his rig and follow her to town. Except that he knew he had responsibilities to take care of first. Best case scenario, it'd be an hour before he could get away from the marina. But he could check in on her by phone. He'd give her enough time to make it to town before he sent her a text. Garret wasn't much into texting, but it seemed less intrusive than phoning her. He certainly didn't want to worry her. He could tell she was already feeling pretty anxious. And why not? He would have to make it seem like he just wanted to keep tabs on her. No big deal. She didn't need to know that he couldn't get her off his mind—and not just for safety concerns either.

Seeing Wade now being questioned by the police, Garret decided to go over to listen in. He had some questions he wanted to ask Wade, too. He watched as Wade told the police that he pretty much knew nothing about any of this. And that wasn't surprising since Garret had barely had a chance to talk to him this morning. Still he was curious as to whether Wade had observed anything out of the ordinary in the past several days. Something that hindsight might spotlight.

Growing bored with the line of questioning, Garret went to check on a boat in the shop. The new employee, Kent Jones, had been assigned to it, but from what Garret could see, Kent's work wasn't only slipshod, it was absent—just like Kent. The inboard motor looked pretty much the same as when he'd started on it last week.

Seeing that the police were all leaving, Garret let Rocky out of the dog run and then headed over to the marina store. Calling out for Wade, he discovered him restocking sodas into the small cooler by the cash register. "Have you seen Kent today?" Garret asked him.

Wade shook his head. "I don't recall seeing him since Wednesday."

"And he hasn't called in sick?"

"I haven't heard a word from him."

"Have you seen him around your apartment building? He still lives there, right?"

"As far as I know." Wade frowned.

"He's a good friend of yours, isn't he?" Garret studied Wade closely. Wade was the one who had brought Kent on board.

Wade looked uncertain as he leaned down to scratch Rocky behind the ears.

"I mean, you did recommend him for the job, didn't you?" Garret waited, feeling impatient.

"Yeah, well, Kent moved into my apartment complex a while back," Wade told him. "But I wouldn't call him a friend exactly. Not a *good* friend, anyway. I mean he was sure friendly and everything—at first. I hadn't known him that long, but he kept telling me he was looking for a boat mechanic job, talking like he was real experienced, the best thing since sliced bread. And when Larry moved inland, I told Kent about the job here. You said you needed a new mechanic."

"Right…" Garret rubbed his chin. "So you didn't know Kent that well?"

"Not really." Wade frowned. "Why?"

"Because I'm not so sure about him. And when I checked out his work on that Chris Craft inboard just now, well, I'm pretty disappointed. I think I'll have to let him go." If Kent hadn't left already—like Garret suspected.

"Man, I'm sorry, Garret." Wade slowly shook his head. "I believed him when he told me he was good with boats. He talked it up big."

Garret studied Wade. He'd been working at the marina for several years and Garret had never had a reason to doubt him…till now.

"Do you think Kent might've been setting you up?" Garret asked. "You know, befriending you just to get hired here?"

Wade ran his fingers through his short blond hair. "Yeah, maybe so. To be honest, the more I got to know Kent, the less I trusted him. You know?"

Garret just nodded. He was tempted to say more, but he wasn't a hundred percent certain he could trust Wade. Especially considering his lack of judgment in recommending a guy he barely knew. "Well, just keep your eyes open," he told him. "Something's going on around here. And, despite what Detective Greene said about that gunshot being random this morning, I'm convinced it was intentional."

Wade glanced down at Rocky. "Want to leave Rocky out to roam? Just to help keep watch?"

"Good idea. But if you need to, feel free to put him in his run." Garret held up his phone. "And if you see anything the least bit suspicious, let me know. And if anything crazy happens, don't hesitate to call 911."

Wade's eyes grew big. "Yeah, sure. I will."

"And if Kent shows up for work, just play dumb, okay?"

"What'd'ya mean?"

"Don't let on that he's history here. Let me take care of that later."

"No problem." Wade looked relieved.

"Although I doubt he'll be back."

As Garret went to talk to Sharon, his house-keeper, he felt fairly certain that Wade was telling the truth about Kent. He probably didn't know the newcomer that well. But that didn't excuse Wade from recommending him for a job. And, although Garret didn't plan to tell Wade as much, he suspected that Kent was involved in this recent crime spree somehow. Maybe it was just paranoid suspicion…or maybe something more. But he planned to get to the bottom of it.

"Hey, Sharon." Garret waved to the middle-aged woman. He tried not to look too disgruntled as she took one last quick puff on her cigarette before she ground it out under the heel of her worn tennis shoe. She knew about his nonsmoking policy on marina property.

"Hey, Garret." She picked up the half-full laundry basket and hurried to meet him. "What happened this morning, anyway? Cindy—you know, my friend who lives down the road from here—she called me to say the place was crawling with cops. What's going on?"

He explained the "random" gunshot, but Sharon frowned. "A random gunshot that busts through your sliding door? With you sitting right in front of it? That doesn't sound very random to me."

He made a half smile. "Yeah, I know."

She glanced over her shoulder. "Is it safe here?"

"I hope so." He frowned. "But I can't guarantee anything. So if you feel the least bit unsafe, feel free to leave. I've been warning the guests about the situation and, although the police are calling it random, I've told them they're free to check out with a full refund for the remainder of the weekend. So far no one has taken me up on it."

"Then you'll still need housekeeping," she declared.

"Of course. But you're not afraid to be here?"

She shrugged. "Nah. Don't see why anyone would want to mess with me."

"Okay. If you're sure."

She grinned. "Besides, I kinda thrive on

excitement. Just watched three reruns of *CSI* last night."

He couldn't help but laugh. "Anyway, I'd like you to help me get Cabin A put together for a guest." He explained his plan and, promising her holiday wages, was glad when she eagerly agreed.

As Garret headed to the storage shed for tools, he wondered if it was irresponsible for him to let guests and employees remain here. Maybe he should've just turned them all out. But he knew his employees needed their pay. And where would his guests go?

Besides, wasn't that kind of like letting the crooks win? How was that right?

And, like Lieutenant Conrad had told him earlier this morning, Larsson's Marina, like the newspaper office and Rory's house, was on the police's radar now. Michael had even suggested they might post a cruiser nearby. Especially if Megan stayed on there. Fortunately, Michael was starting to understand that Megan, because of her relationship with Rory, might very well be in danger, too. Too bad Detective Greene wasn't as easily convinced. Whether it was youth, inexperience or just plain arrogance, Garret had to agree with Megan. Detective Greene continued to foster the attitude that all these recent occurrences were simply random coincidences—and it was most irritating.

As he carried the paint and a few other things back to Cabin A, he sent Megan a text. He didn't say much, just that he was checking in to be sure she was okay. Going into the cabin, he looked around, doing a quick mental inventory of the things that needed to get put into place to make the cabin more livable. But first he needed to board up the broken sliding door in his own cabin. And now that the police were gone, Garret decided it might be time to strap on his own gun and holster.

As Garret used his screw gun to secure a piece of plywood over the shot-out glass door, he didn't really like the feeling of wearing a gun holster along with his tool belt. Truth be told, Garret wasn't overly fond of firearms. Not like his grandfather had been. Sure, he'd enjoyed target-shooting with Grandpa. And as a young teen he'd complied with his grandpa's wishes to take gun safety classes. He'd even attained his concealed carry permit one summer while working at the marina during his college days.

But after Grandpa died, his grandmother had convinced Garret that it was now his responsibility—as marina manager—to ensure the safety and well-being of the guests and boat owners. She had ceremoniously handed over his grandfather's holster and Ruger handgun. "To use for any uninvited, unsavory characters who show up at our marina," she had solemnly told him. "Not to kill them, of course, but just to keep them from hurting anyone."

So Garret had agreed to keep a firearm, but for the most part, he'd kept it locked up in his grandfather's gun safe. It was only after listening to Rory this past month, hearing his theories about the criminal activity along the waterfront that Garret got more serious about firearm protection. Garret had no doubts that there was some drug-running going on around and about Cape Perpetua. Two weeks ago he'd had an encounter with a drunken boat captain threatening a fisherman. The incident had pushed him to purchase a small gun safe, which he'd secured to the floor of his SUV. At the time it had seemed a little extreme, but after what happened last night, he was glad he'd done it.

Hearing a buzz on his phone, he checked it to see that Megan had responded to his text, announcing she was just fine. Feeling relieved, he put the last screw into the plywood and decided to spend some time working on Cabin A. At least, when she came back here, she would feel welcome. And he would feel relieved to know that she was nearby.

It was a little past noon when he finished his

work in Cabin A. He paused to look around. The baseboard, window and door trim were complete, the bathroom and closet doors were installed, the curtains were hung, the shower rod and bathroom accessories were in place. With Sharon's help, the bed was properly made and she was just starting to apply the pale aqua-blue paint to the bathroom walls.

Garret was just putting his tools away when he heard his phone jingling. Seeing that it was Megan's number, he eagerly answered. Perhaps she'd be interested in getting some lunch.

"Hey, Megan," he said cheerfully. "What's up?"

"Not much." Her voice sounded a little uneasy. "It's just that I'm at Dad's house."

"You went there alone?" he asked. "Are there any police around?"

"Michael was supposed to meet me here, but he hasn't arrived yet."

"So you're there by yourself?" he asked.

"Uh…yeah."

"Well, don't go inside, Megan. Wait for Michael."

"That's my plan."

"You know I would've been glad to go through the house with you."

"I know, but Michael was supposed to be here so I felt safe. But I probably should've waited."

"It'll take me a few minutes, but I'll be right—"

"I hate to bother you, Garret. You've already been such a help."

"Never mind about that. In the meantime, do me a favor and get out of there. Maybe you could just meet me in town and we could—"

"Yeah, I was just locking the door. I was about to go inside, and I got this, well, an uneasy feeling. That's when I thought to myself, it's time to phone a friend." She made a nervous-sounding laugh. "I thought I could just talk to you as I went inside, you know?"

"Well, if you have a bad feeling you should get out of there." He set his tool belt on the workbench.

"Just what I'm doing if I could get this stupid door locked again. My hands are kind of jittery."

"I understand." He kept his voice calm, hoping to reassure her. "So I was just wondering if you wanted to get some lunch. I still have some stuff to tell you about your dad and I thought—" His words were interrupted by a blood-curdling scream. "Megan?" he yelled into the phone. "Are you okay?"

The scream continued, followed by scuffling sounds—and then the connection broke completely. Nothing but dead air.

Garret was already running toward the marina parking lot. As he ran, he dialed 911, telling the dispatcher to send emergency help to Rory's house. "It's Megan McCallister," he said breathlessly. "She's in trouble."

NINE

Megan ran full speed to the nearest neighbor. With each step she prayed that Luella Martin would be home.

Pounding on Mrs. Martin's door, she screamed in terror. "It's Megan McCallister, please, let me in!"

The door opened with Luella staring at her in shock—but before Megan explained, she leaped through the door, slammed it shut and locked the dead bolt. "A man," she gasped, "in Dad's house. He came at me."

Luella grabbed Megan by the hand, guiding her into a bedroom before closing and locking the door. Then she hurried toward the landline phone on the bedside table. "I'll call 911."

As Luella grabbed up her phone, Megan checked her pockets for her own phone and realized that she must've lost it when she tumbled down the front stairs. She'd been approaching her father's house when she saw someone lurking in the shadows of her dad's porch. Unable to speak, she'd backed away from him. But when he charged her, she'd screamed and stumbled backward on the porch steps, barely getting up in time to escape the intruder and run to her father's neighbor.

Hearing Luella talking to the 911 dispatcher, Megan held out her hand. "I should probably tell them what happened."

Luella nodded and handed her the phone.

"It's Rory McCallister's house," Megan said in a shrill voice, still trying to calm herself as she gave them the address. "It looks like the house has been ransacked," she explained. "The intruder was dressed in dark clothing. I caught him by surprise, but he chased after me." She explained who she was and where she was and that she thought they were safe, and continued to answer questions.

"I need to call Garret," she told Luella as she hung up. "He's probably freaking out." She told the woman about the disrupted phone call. But as she stared at the numbers on the landline phone, she realized that she didn't know Garret's number. It was saved in the contacts of her missing cell phone. And the business card he'd given her was in her purse, which was locked in her car.

"There's the police now," Luella told Megan

as the first cruiser came down the road. "Do you think the burglar is still around?"

"I doubt it." Megan frowned as they both looked out the side window facing her dad's house. Then suddenly she broke down into tears.

"You poor thing." Luella gathered Megan into her arms. "You lose your daddy and then someone breaks into his house. Not just once, but twice. It's so wrong."

"Why are they doing this?" Megan asked between tears. "What is wrong with people?"

"I don't know, honey. But sometimes it just feels like the whole world is spinning out of control." Luella reached for a tissue from the bedside table, handing it to Megan.

"I know." Megan used it to wipe her tears and blow her nose. "Cape Perpetua just isn't the same anymore."

"That's what your daddy kept saying." Luella sighed. "But it seemed like nobody wanted to listen."

"Did he tell you about it?"

"Not so much." Luella reached for another tissue, blotting her own eyes. "Bless his heart, I don't think he liked to worry me. Sometimes we'd share some coffee or lemonade and he'd start to tell me about something, but then he'd stop. Almost like he didn't want me to know about the troubles plaguing this town."

Megan nodded. As sweet as Luella Martin was—and a good neighbor—she had a tendency to get easily worked up. At least that's what Dad used to say. To be fair to the elderly woman, Luella had been relatively calm when Megan had burst into her house.

"Oh, my." Luella let out a little sob. "This town is going to miss Rory McCallister."

"I know." Megan looked out the window to see there were two cop cars in the driveway now. "I better go talk to them," she told Luella as she reached for the bedroom door. "Thanks so much for your help. Make sure you keep your doors locked. Although I doubt they'll be troubling you."

Luella frowned. "That might be true, but I think I'll call my daughter just the same. See if I can visit her for a few days."

"That's an excellent idea." Megan nodded as she went for the front door, pausing to thank and hug the old woman again. "Enjoy your time with your daughter." She wanted to add *you never know how many more times you'll get* but stopped herself. No need to trouble poor Luella any more than she already was.

Relieved to see that Lieutenant Conrad was one of the cops already standing outside the house, Megan hurried over to join him. "Get back behind here," he told her as he led her to the rear of an emergency vehicle. "Was the man armed?"

"I honestly don't know," she confessed. "When he charged toward me, I just ran. But there were no gunshots. My guess is he's gone by now."

"We have to be cautious just the same."

"Why are they doing this?" she asked him. "What's really going on?"

"I'm not really sure. But your dad had some crazy hunches." He nodded toward the house. "Looks like they're going in."

She looked at the front porch, where three cops were positioning themselves to enter. "What about the back of the house?" she asked Michael.

"A couple guys are back there already," he told her.

"I'm guessing they're too late."

"You're probably right. But maybe we can collect some evidence."

Megan glanced around. "Is Detective Greene here?"

"Not yet. But he'll be by after his lunch break."

Megan controlled herself from rolling her eyes. "Michael, just between you and me, do you think he knows what he's doing?"

"He's got good credentials."

"But not much in the way of experience, right?"

Michael gave a half smile.

"Why didn't they pick someone like you to be the detective?" she asked.

He shrugged. "Not sure I'd want it. I'm looking forward to retirement in a couple of years. Time to start taking it easy."

About a mile down the graveled road, she could see a familiar-looking SUV approaching fast, leaving a trail of dust behind it. "Uh-oh," she said.

"What's wrong?" Michael went into high alert as he followed her gaze. "Who's that?"

"Garret Larsson. I was talking to him on my phone when the intruder charged at me. I screamed then dropped my phone while he was still on the other end. Poor Garret probably thinks I'm toast by now."

"He's going pretty fast."

"You won't ticket him, will you?"

Michael shrugged. "Not this time."

She walked down the driveway toward the road, waving to Garret in an attempt to show him she was okay. Then jogging, she went up to meet him, jumping inside his SUV and explaining everything.

"Did you find your phone yet?" he asked.

"Not yet. I should probably wait until the police give me the green light."

"I was worried about letting you go off by yourself," he told her as he parked behind the police vehicles. "But if I'd known you were coming here, I would've dropped everything to come with you, Megan."

"I didn't think it would be a problem. I mean, Michael was supposed to meet me. And it was broad daylight."

"But then you got that bad feeling?" He turned off the engine.

"I felt uneasy," she confessed.

"Was it what you'd call women's intuition?" he asked as they got out.

She shrugged. "Yeah, maybe."

"Aren't you supposed to listen to that?" He peered curiously at her.

"I guess so."

Michael was coming over to join them now. "It looks like the intruder is gone. But the place is a mess inside. The team's gathering evidence now."

"Can I look around the porch area?" she asked. "I dropped my phone over there."

"Didn't you say the intruder followed you out the front door?"

"Yeah, but—"

"Then you better let the team look for footprints first."

She bit her lip. "Yeah...sure."

"Do you think it's the same guy from the newspaper office?" Garret asked her.

"I really don't know." She tried to remember. "It happened so fast. I was so shocked, I just took off running."

"Good thing, too," Garret told her.

"He seemed similar. Dark clothes. Average height. Medium build." She closed her eyes, trying to pull up that face again. "But his skin seemed darker. Tanned. Almost Hispanic. But it was more of an impression. I wouldn't stake my life on it."

Garret turned to Michael. "I have some things I need to tell Megan about. Things that Rory told me. I think maybe you should hear them, too." He glanced at his watch. "Have you guys had lunch? I'm starving."

The three agreed to meet at The Chowder House for lunch, and Garret insisted Megan ride with him. He could tell she was rattled and tired—and he had a strong urge to take care of her.

"Were you able to figure out everything with your car this morning?" he asked as he drove.

"Yeah. The tires are all covered by AAA. Then I noticed Arthur was working in the newspaper office so I went inside and talked to him a while. I asked him to notify the other employees that they'll be laid off with pay until further notice."

"Further notice being...?"

"I'll have to let them know the paper is shutting down and that I'll list it for sale after Memorial Day."

"That's pretty tough news."

"Believe me, I know. And it's not easy."

"No, I wouldn't think it would be." Garret refrained from pointing out how this decision would've broken her father's heart. And, really, who could blame her for wanting to close it down and get out of here? So far Cape Perpetua hadn't been exactly welcoming.

"Then Michael called to see how I was. He asked about Dad's memorial service. So I called the church and reserved the date. It'll be at three o'clock on Wednesday afternoon."

"Same day the newspaper came out."

"Yeah. I thought Dad would like that. It'll be at his church. Pastor Jackson has been really helpful. He's handling a lot of it for me. Such a great guy."

"That's good."

"But I still need to go to the mortuary. Dad sent me a packet a couple of years ago. I never really looked at it...never expected to need it so soon. But it was for a plan at Riverside Funeral Home. I left a message with the director that I'd stop by today." She let out a tired sigh, leaning back into the seat.

"You're probably exhausted."

"I kind of am."

"Maybe you can have some downtime after lunch."

She sat up straighter now. "I don't expect any downtime until this whole thing is wrapped up."

"Wrapped up?" He eyed her curiously. "What exactly do you mean by that?"

"I want to know how Dad died—and if it's related to all this other stuff. I want to get to the bottom of it."

"I think that's what Rory had been trying to do, too," he said glumly. "But, as he found out, it wasn't that easy."

"So you do know what he was working on?" She looked intently at him. "And you never even told me?"

"If you remember correctly, I started to tell you a number of times. But it seems like we're always getting interrupted by things like stray bullets, killers and such."

"Even so." She sounded aggravated, and he felt a bit guilty.

"It's not like I really know anything specifically. Rory didn't exactly spill the beans. But I've been putting some things together—my hunch has been growing."

"So you're going to tell Michael and me about your hunch?"

He nodded as he turned next to the bridge, pulling up in front of the rustic building that housed the old café. "That's my plan. Unless someone attempts to blow this place up while we're talking."

"That's so not funny."

"I wasn't joking." He looked cautiously around as he led her into the funky old restaurant. "I'm watching my back pretty carefully now. You should be, too."

"I know." She looked at the low wooden building. "I haven't been here in years. Dad used to bring me a lot. But as a teenager, I started turning my nose up at it." She sighed as they went inside. "What a little fool I was."

He chuckled. "Chalk it up to adolescence."

Relieved that nothing seemed changed, Megan paused by the big bulletin board by the door. The Bragging Board was where fishermen tacked their trophy photos up. "Look." She pointed to one of her dad with a gigantic fish and a huge grin. "That lingcod was nearly sixty pounds," she told Garret.

He chuckled. "Too bad Rory didn't like lingcod."

"I know. He donated it to the soup kitchen.

Only reason he didn't throw it back was because it was photo worthy."

Garret pointed to a booth in the corner. "That okay?"

"Yeah." She nodded to the door. "Here comes Michael."

After they were settled and orders placed, Garret was just starting to explain what Rory had been working on when Michael suddenly stood. Pointing out the window that looked out to the bridge and river, he asked, "Does that look like this morning's boat?"

Megan and Garret both turned to see. "Yes!" Megan exclaimed. Then, suddenly afraid, she asked, "Are we in danger?"

"I don't know, but I plan to find out." Michael was reaching for his phone. "But you kids stay away from the windows."

"Need help?" Garret offered.

"I don't think so." Michael was heading for the door. "I just want to tip off the coast guard. Maybe they've got a cutter nearby."

As Michael went outside, Megan and Garret hovered behind a shelf filled with tourist trinkets. It worked as a divider to block them from the window.

"What's up?" the waitress asked with curiosity.

Garret quickly explained, urging her and the

other restaurant workers to remain in the kitchen until they got the all-clear. But as Garret was peeking around the side of the trinket shelf, Megan felt herself trembling uncontrollably. She tried to make herself believe it was low blood sugar, something that happened occasionally when she skipped a meal. But she knew what it really was.

Plain old ordinary fear.

TEN

Michael returned after a few minutes, explaining that he'd called the Coast Guard and that a cutter was on the way.

"Do you think that's the same boat that took a shot at you this morning?" he asked Megan.

She shrugged. "Hard to tell. So many of these fishing boats look alike."

"And there are plenty out there," Garret added.

"We'll let the coast guard check it out." Michael shrugged. "Chances are it was nothing. I think we're all just on high alert. Probably a good thing. Meanwhile…" He turned to the waitress with a wry grin. "Our order up yet?"

"Have it out to you in two shakes of a lamb's tail." She hurried back to the kitchen.

After they returned to the table, Michael reminded Garret that he was about to tell them his theory about Rory.

"Right." Garret waited as the waitress set down their order then jumped in. "I probably won't tell this chronologically, but then you already know some of the background, Michael." He glanced at Megan. "Although you might not. So, anyway, Rory had been part of the opposition against the opening of the casino."

Michael nodded. "Everyone in town knew that."

"So did I," Megan told them.

"He did a lot of investigating of it—back during the planning stages. His first concern had been that the casino would lure in people who couldn't afford to gamble."

"Yes," she said eagerly. "I remember the headline he used—*Casinos are Weapons of Cash Deduction*."

Garret continued. "The more Rory looked into the whole thing, the more concerned he was for a number of other issues, too, He wrote a number of exposés about other casinos. He followed the money trail in an attempt to inform readers of how most of the casino profits went straight back to Las Vegas, by way of the developers, ending up primarily in the pockets of organized crime."

"Right," she said. "Dad told me about that, too. But the way I understood it, he worked with the members of the tribe to ensure that they didn't get taken advantage of like that. And when they finally settled on a developer, they negotiated for a fairer portion of the profits."

"That's the way I understood it," Michael told her. "And to be fair, after they got used to the idea, most of the town has been positive about the casino. Not only has it provided jobs, it's stimulated the tourist economy, as well. Most folks feel like it's a win-win."

"Except for when you lose," Garret said wryly.

"Well, I think Dad was right to help the tribe," Megan said quietly.

"Yeah, it seemed that way in the beginning," Garret said. "But things aren't always what they seem. About a year ago, after a conversation with the tribal council, Rory started helping them track what was going on. There were suspicions that they were being taken advantage of. Rory confided to me that he was convinced the developers weren't divvying up the money fairly." He frowned. "To be honest, I didn't quite buy it. But lately, with all that's gone on, I've been giving it some thought. What if Rory was right? With all those computerized games and all that money flying around, wouldn't it be easy for some of the money to slip through the cracks?" His brow creased. "For all we know, it could've been millions."

"So Rory believed millions of dollars were going to the developers?" Michael frowned doubtfully.

"Where else?" Garret asked him.

"Who are the developers?" Megan asked.

"The Marco brothers," Michael told her. "Tony and Vince Marco."

"Are they related to that new restaurant?" Megan asked. "Marco's on the Waterfront? I just saw it today. Pretty swanky."

"Swanky doesn't even begin to describe it," Garret said. "I heard that Tony's wife was in charge of the decor and she pulled out all the stops.

"Anyway," he continued, "Rory suspected that Tony and Vince Marco were skimming from the casino. Not only that, but he believed they have some deep mafia connections. And the restaurant is their way of laundering, not only the casino money, but drug-trafficking money, as well."

"That's a pretty big accusation," Michael said.

"And a dangerous one," Megan added.

"I know." Garret lowered his voice. "Rory was certain that the Marco brothers were involved in a huge drug-trafficking operation, and that they were using our waterfront to do it. Possibly the restaurant, too. For about a month or so Rory sat and counted seafood deliveries, paying attention to the fishing boats using the public docks. In the end, he was convinced that it just didn't add up."

"These are all very interesting theories," Michael said, "but did Rory have any solid proof?"

"I'm sure he did." Garret glanced at Megan. "In fact, I'm worried that might even be why he died. Someone wanted to shut him up."

"So it was *not* natural causes," she declared.

"I didn't want to believe he'd been murdered. But after this recent crime spree, well, it's like the writing on the wall."

"So are you seriously suggesting that the Marco brothers murdered Rory?" Michael's brows drew together.

"I'm suggesting they might've hired a hit man." Garret slowly shook his head. "And I'm kicking myself for not seeing it coming."

"What do you mean?" Megan demanded.

"Last week Rory told me that he felt he had the goods on the Marcos. I brought him some fish and chips for lunch and he had this big yellow envelope sitting on his desk. He patted it and told me it contained everything he needed to write an exposé that would blow everything sky high."

"So is that what these break-ins are all about?" Megan asked him. "Is that what they're looking for? The yellow envelope?"

Garret pursed his lips. "That's my guess. I didn't put everything together until this morning when I saw Rory's Jeep broken into. That's when I remembered the envelope—and something else."

"What?" both Michael and Megan asked eagerly.

"Rory mentioned that he didn't plan to break his story until after Memorial Day weekend. Didn't want to give the town a black eye with all these tourists in town. But that wasn't all." He lowered his voice again. "Rory wanted to interview Tony and Vince."

"Are you serious?" Megan felt sick inside. "Dad wanted to interview those criminals?"

"He was a newsman," Garret told her. "You know what that means."

Megan did know. As a journalist, she sometimes placed herself in harm's way to get a story. But this was her dad. Why had he wanted to engage with mafia men like that?

"That's quite a story." Michael blotted his mouth with a paper napkin. "But without proof, it's just that. A story." He scowled at Garret. "Even so, I don't know why you didn't tell the police about this sooner."

"I'm not sure I trusted everyone on the force just yet. I mean I trust you, Michael, but the Cape Perpetua police have had some problems recently."

Michael nodded grimly. "Yes, that's true."

"And that's probably why Rory was being careful, too."

"But we've cleaned up the police force," Michael pointed out.

"Back to the yellow envelope," Megan said eagerly. "If that contains the proof, we need to find it."

"Yes, but after all the break-ins..." Michael sighed. "The newspaper office, Rory's house, his Jeep... Even his boat is missing. Chances are it's in the wrong hands."

"But what if they didn't find it yet?" she pressed. "That would explain why they haven't given up."

"Where else is there to look?" Garret asked.

"I don't know." Megan shook her head. She really didn't know. Where else might Dad have hidden something that important?

"Well, I've got to get to the station." Michael slid out of the booth. "What you say makes sense, Garret. But like I said, without proof..."

"I know." Garret stood.

"We'll get the proof," Megan declared.

"How?" the men both asked.

"I know my dad," she said firmly. "If that yellow envelope contained information that was that important, he would hide it somewhere that no one could find it. I intend to find it."

"But if the crooks are still looking for it, you'll be in danger," Michael warned.

"Then you better send some cops to back me up," she told him. "Because I plan to keep looking."

"I'll do the best we can," Michael said as they went outside. "But this is a holiday weekend. Our force is already spread pretty thin."

"I'll back her up," Garret told Michael as he tossed some cash on the table. "Let me get this."

"Thanks." Megan smiled at Garret. "For everything."

"Keep me informed of your whereabouts," Michael told Megan as they headed for the door.

"I will. And I appreciate that you're taking this seriously now."

"Of course I'm taking it seriously," he assured her as they walked to their cars. "Rory was a good friend to me, too."

"I know." She waited as Garret opened the passenger door of his SUV for her.

Michael had the door of his police car open, too. "You both need to be on high alert," he told them. "And like I said, keep me—"

His words were cut off by a loud boom, but before Megan could see what had happened, Garret had knocked her to the ground.

"Wh-what was that?" She was on her knees in the gravel.

"A gun!" Garret removed his phone from his pocket and then his gun from the holster, looking right and left and staying down low. "Are you okay?"

"Yeah." She felt her heart pounding like it was going to leap from her chest. "Just scared half to death."

"Michael," Garret called out. "Lieutenant Conrad? You okay?"

Megan leaned down to peer beneath the SUV and over to the police cruiser where Michael, like them, had gotten down on the gravel parking lot. But instead of being on his haunches, he was lying down and his eyes were closed. But it was the dark pool of blood gathering around him that made Megan scream. "Michael's been shot!"

ELEVEN

"I've got to go help him." Garret shoved his phone to her. "Stay down and call 911."

"But you could get shot," she said in horror.

"He needs help," Garret said as he crouched low, making his way around the front of his car. "Call 911!" he yelled again.

With shaking fingers, she tapped those three numbers again, quickly telling the dispatcher, "There's an officer down!" She gave their location and answered the questions. "Please hurry. Michael needs medical attention now."

"Help is on the way. Do you know where the shot came from?"

"The shooter might be on the water. You should call the coast guard for backup."

The dispatcher kept Megan on the line, assuring her that help was coming, and asking for updates on Lieutenant Conrad.

"How's Michael?" Megan yelled to Garret.

"He's breathing. But bleeding a lot. I'm trying to stop it."

Megan relayed this to the dispatcher.

"Tell him to apply direct pressure. Paramedics are just three minutes away now."

Megan yelled this information to him.

"I am," he called back. "Hang on, Michael," he said urgently. "Pray for him, Megan."

"I am," she yelled back. And with the dispatcher still on the other end, Megan began to pray, begging God to spare Michael's life.

Michael was pale when the paramedics took over for Garret, but at least he was conscious now. "Hang in there, buddy." Garret stepped away, feeling reluctant to leave his side. "You're in good hands. And we'll be praying for you."

Garret felt a tap on his shoulder and turned to see Detective Greene.

"I need to talk to you," he told Garret.

With his hands still covered in blood, Garret followed the detective to a nearby bench. As he sat, he noticed another cop questioning Megan.

Trying to be helpful, Garret proceeded to answer the fairly standard but not terribly clever questions. He confirmed where they'd all been standing and how he'd found Michael on the ground.

"Looks to me he took the shot from his left

side, which tells me that, if the shooter wasn't on a boat down in the river, he was probably on the bridge. Although you'd think someone might've spotted a gunman up there. But I'm sure your experts can figure out the bullet trajectory and distance better than I can."

"Of course." Then the detective questioned why Garret and Megan had been here with the lieutenant in the first place. "Or was this just a random encounter?"

"We met here to have some lunch and to discuss the case."

"What case?" Detective Greene scowled.

Garret stared down at his bloody hands. Seriously—was this junior detective that dense? Or was he simply playing games? Garret locked eyes with him. "I think you know what case."

"What are you suggesting?"

"Suggesting?" Garret tried to stifle his irritation. "You are aware of the recent crimes, aren't you, Detective Greene? Well, this shooting was obviously related."

"I don't see anything obvious about it. And even if it did involve the same perpetrators as the other incidents, why would they want to shoot a cop?" His tone sounded irritatingly nonchalant.

Garret took in a deep breath. "Why would *anyone* want to shoot *anyone*? And, for that matter, why should we assume the shooter was aiming at Michael? For all we know, he could've been aiming at Megan or me and the gunman was just a bad shot. Or maybe it was meant to be a warning shot. I don't know." Garret glared at him. "You're the detective, why don't *you* figure it out?"

"Are you trying to win this week's hostile witness award?"

As Garret stood, he thought maybe he was. "If you'll excuse me, Detective, I'd like to check on Megan." Then without giving him a chance to detain him further, Garret went inside the restaurant where Megan was talking to a uniformed officer.

"You ready to go?" he abruptly asked her.

She looked up in surprise then pointed at him. "Sure, but maybe you should wash up first."

He looked back down at his hands. "Yeah, good idea."

The waitress's eyes grew large as Garret went back to the men's room. Good thing he'd left a generous tip. As he used dampened paper towels to blot his friend's blood from his shirt, he tried to gauge his reaction to Detective Greene. It wasn't that he believed the detective was a bad cop. But his arrogance made him seem like a stupid cop. And in some ways, stupid was not much different than bad.

He remembered Megan's resolve to find

Rory's big yellow envelope. Now his mind was made up. Together they would find that envelope. Together they would take down the Marco brothers. If the police could help them, fine. If not, they would do it on their own.

He threw the paper towels away and went out to Megan. "Let's go." He took her by the arm as he led her to the door, giving a careful glance all around before exiting. Despite the number of cops still investigating the area, Garret knew better than to assume they were safe.

"You seem to be in a hurry."

"That's because we've got work to do." He opened the door for her, his eyes still roaming the bridge and the river, and watching for anything suspicious as he hurried over to the driver's side.

"Work?" she asked as he got inside and buckled his seat belt.

"Like you said." He started the engine. "We're going to find that yellow envelope."

"Good. But maybe you should change first. That looks pretty scary, Garret."

He looked down at his damp blood-stained shirt and nodded. "Yeah. Good idea."

As he turned onto the main road, he started to lay out his plan. "I think we should start with the newspaper office. You interrupted your mugger's search last night, so it's possible the envelope is still there. Hopefully well hidden, because I agree with what you told Michael. Your dad wouldn't leave something that important just lying around."

"Especially if he'd interviewed the Marco brothers." She shuddered. "They sound so horrible. Do you think he really met with them?"

"He sounded pretty determined, Megan. Knowing Rory, I'm guessing he did."

"Yeah, me, too."

"If we don't find the envelope at the newspaper, we'll head back to his house. The good news there is that you interrupted the intruder again. Hopefully, no one's been back."

"And I'll let the police know," she told him. "Scott Barnett is a second-lieutenant and a good friend of Michael's. He seems like a really nice guy—and smart, too. I told him what Michael told me about providing backup or surveillance or whatever. Anyway, Scott gave me his business card, saying I could call him with my whereabouts and he'd do his best to get someone out there or come himself."

As Garret drove, Megan called Scott, informing him of their plan. After she hung up, she suggested they pray for Michael. Once again, Garret felt like Megan was his kind of girl. He could barely comprehend how, after spending less than twenty-four hours with her, he felt seriously attracted. And protective, too. It wasn't a superficial feeling, either. Not because of her good looks—although she was truly beautiful. But it was her whole persona—a mixture of intelligent independence and sweet vulnerability—that pulled him in. She was just the sort of woman he'd always imagined spending his life with. But up until now, he'd never met a woman quite like this. Some had come close, but he'd never felt quite like this before.

"You know, Megan," he began as he parked next to the marina shop, cautiously looking around, "I'd like to make a suggestion."

"A suggestion?" She turned to him and as he looked into her eyes, he thought of how the river looked early in the morning—sort of green, blue, gray. Enchanting.

"Yeah, I'm concerned at how dangerous this thing has gotten. I wonder if you'd consider going home, back to Seattle I mean, until things settle down."

"Are you kidding?" Her eyes flashed with anger.

"Not at all."

"I have no intention of leaving Cape Perpetua, Garret. Not until I get to the bottom of this. And there's Dad's burial arrangements, the memorial service and—"

"I know. But those things could wait. I know if Rory could talk to us, he would agree with me."

She pursed her lips, as if considering this. "I'm not so sure about that. My dad raised me to be strong—to think for myself. Don't misunderstand me, Garret, I'm no shrinking violet. I can hold my own. And I really don't appreciate you thinking you can just ship me off like I'm the little lady and—"

"Okay, okay." He held up his hands as if to surrender. "I figured it was worth a try." He gave a meek smile. "And it was only because I care about you, Megan. I don't want to see you get hurt."

She softened slightly. "Sorry to go ballistic on you. And I appreciate that you care about me." She looked into his eyes. "I care about you, too. But I've learned to be tough. As a journalist, I'm used to jostling alongside the boys' club, elbowing my way in to get a good story. I don't usually shirk back." She sighed. "Although I'll admit that losing Dad, well, it has taken a little bit of the wind out of my sails."

Garret made another quick look around the marina, but all looked normal. Wade was on the dock, coiling up some ropes. Sharon was just emerging from the laundry room with a basket of fresh linens. And Rocky was bounding over toward them.

As he got out of the SUV, he stooped to pet Rocky then called out to Wade, waving him over to them.

"Hey, man, what happened to you?" Wade stared at Garret with a shocked expression. "Are you okay?"

Reminded of his bloody shirt, Garret gave Wade a condensed explanation then introduced him to Megan. "She'll be staying in Cabin A for a few days. Can you get her the key?"

"You got it."

"Any excitement around here while we were gone?" he asked Wade.

"Nope. Business as usual."

"Good." Garret turned to Megan. "Your luggage is in your cabin. Just make yourself at home. I'll come by after I clean up." He made one more look around. "Just make sure you lock the door, okay?"

Megan was pleasantly surprised when she entered Cabin A. Someone had been busy in here since she'd left it this morning. But like Garret had asked, she locked the door, even latching the recently installed chain lock, before she looked around to see that the room looked ready for occupancy.

After admiring her new digs, she decided to freshen up her appearance. Part of her felt silly for even caring about her looks—another part of her wanted Garret to like what he saw. She was just finishing up when she heard someone knocking on the door. The sound put her on high alert again. With a shaky hand, she reached for her purse, digging for her phone—just in case— except her phone wasn't there!

TWELVE

Garret began to feel uneasy as he waited for Megan to come to the door. Was something wrong? "Megan?" he called. "It's just me."

She opened the door with a relieved expression. "Sorry. I sort of freaked when I heard the noise."

"Maybe it's not a good idea for you to stay here alone."

"And I still don't have my phone," she reminded him.

"I spoke to Scott Barnett. He suggested it would be easier for the police to protect just one house." He looked around the cabin. "Do you mind moving into mine?"

"Not at all." She looked relieved. "Let me go pack up my stuff."

As he helped carry her bags to the main house, his phone rang. When he answered it, Scott Barnett was on the other end.

"I think we picked up one of the guys," Scott

told Garret. "Can you and Megan meet up with me to give a positive ID?"

"We're on our way." Garret tossed Megan's bags inside then reached for her hand, explaining the situation as they ran back to his car.

Five minutes later they were entering the police station. "This is our first break," Garret told Megan as they head for the reception area. "Maybe the tide's about to turn."

"Go ahead and take a seat," the receptionist told them. "I'll let you know when they're ready for you."

It took about ten minutes before they were let into the area where Scott had managed to round up some guys for a lineup. Megan suddenly felt nervous to think she was about to see this criminal face-to-face. She gave Garret an uneasy look and was relieved when he reached for her hand.

"Just take in a deep breath," he said quietly. "Give yourself time to take a good long look."

She nodded, but as she looked up at the lineup of five men, she realized that she needed no time. She instantly recognized the man in the black hooded sweatshirt and black jeans. "That's him," she told Scott. "In the center."

"No doubts?"

"No doubts." She felt a shiver run down her spine as she stared into the pale pockmarked face, the blank-looking eyes. She almost wondered if he was high on something. "And I'm ninety-nine percent certain that's the same guy who jumped me at the newspaper office last night, too."

"Didn't you say this guy had a knife when you picked him up?" Garret asked Scott.

"That's right." Scott turned to Megan. "Do you think you could recognize the knife?" he asked her.

"I'm not sure about that. But I described the knife to Michael in the police report," she told him. "It looked like a really large hunting knife. You know the kind of blade that's wide with kind of a curve at the tip. And really shiny. But I never saw the handle."

Scott just nodded. "That sounds like his knife. I'll check it against Michael's report. And then we'll start comparing fingerprints from the break-ins."

"Speaking of Michael," Garret asked tentatively, "any word yet?"

"Last I heard he's in surgery. But it sounds like he should be okay."

Garret let out a long sigh, squeezing Megan's hand. "Good to know."

Scott grinned at them. "One down and…how many more to go?"

"At least one more," Megan said. "The darker-skinned man who was in Dad's house."

"Maybe we can get this guy to squeal." Scott waved to the officer who was managing the lineup then turned back to Megan. "You're done here. But stay in touch, okay?"

Megan gave Scott the quick rundown of their plans to go through the newspaper office and then her dad's house.

"Just keep me posted," he told her.

"We will."

As they went back outside, Megan felt a wave of relief washing over her. "I can't believe they got him," she said in wonder. As they stood on the sidewalk, soaking up the afternoon sun, she realized that Garret was still holding her hand. Not that she minded. It was actually quite comforting. And, to be honest, it was more than that, too. She looked up into his teal-blue eyes and sighed. "I feel like I can breathe easier now."

"Good." He smiled warmly down on her. "Now we just need to find that yellow envelope."

She pointed across the street to where the mortuary was located on the corner. "Mind if I pop in there first? I left a message saying I'd be by today."

"Let's go," he said, still holding her hand as they walked across the street.

Megan felt a chill run through her as they went into the big white building, where a man in a dark suit came out to greet them.

"Mr. Bagley." Garret shook his hand, pausing to introduce Megan.

"Oh, Megan." Mr. Bagley grasped her hand. "I'm so sorry for your loss. Your father was a good man. He will be greatly missed in this town."

She thanked him. "I left a message saying I'd be by today. But things got, uh, a little busy. And I seem to have lost my phone."

"That explains why my calls were unanswered," he said as he led them into a paneled office. "Have a seat, please."

After they were seated, he explained that he'd tried to call her several times. "It wasn't that I needed your permission, since your father had already attended to everything, but it is always nice to have contact with the deceased one's closest relatives."

"Yes, I'm sorry to be unavailable."

"So, as I was saying, we have already taken care of your father's final plans. And the remains will be ready to be picked up in time for the ceremony."

"What?" Megan was confused.

"I'm sorry," Mr. Bagley said gently. "I assumed you knew what your father's final wishes were. I asked him to give a copy of his funeral plan to his next of kin. I assume that's you."

"Yes, of course. And he did that. But to be

honest, I never had a chance to really look at it. And, besides, I never thought my dad would die…like this."

"Yes, we never do expect it, do we? That's why it's best to be prepared. Fortunately, your father was prepared."

"Right…" Megan still felt confused. "So his service is Wednesday and—"

"Yes, Pastor Jackson and I have already discussed that. And, like I said, we have a copy of your father's funeral plan and we were aware that he wanted his service to be at his church. And I must agree that's more personal that way. But since the service is on Wednesday, I knew it would be best to schedule the cremation for today. You see, we're closed on Sundays and then Monday is a holiday. So everything here is shut down and, well, it takes a while for the crematory to reach the proper temperatures when we reopen again on Tuesday, and so it was more prudent to take care of the procedure today while the crematory was still—"

"What?" Megan stood up. She could not believe what she had just heard. "What did you just say?"

"Excuse me?" Mr. Bagley's pale brows arched.

Megan stared at him in horror. "Are you saying that you *cremated* my father?"

THIRTEEN

"I'm sorry this is troubling to you, Miss McCallister. But we were only following your father's final wishes," Mr. Bagley calmly told her. "Fulfilling our contractual obligations with him is our primary purpose."

"So you really did it? You cremated him—already?" Megan felt tears coming.

Mr. Bagley clasped his hands together, nodding solemnly. "According to his wishes."

"But what about the autopsy?" she demanded, trying to blink back the tears. "The police promised there would be one—"

"There was one. It was the coroner who called us yesterday to—"

"But no one called me. Did they perform toxicology and—"

"I can't answer to those details. But I do know that the coroner completed his report. That's why he called to arrange for a transport." As Mr. Bagley stood, his face remained serene. "Everything was done accordingly. Nothing had been done out of order. I'm so very sorry that this has taken you by—"

"I just didn't expect this. It's not how I—I—" Megan's voice cracked as she broke into tears.

"Losing a family member is never easy for anyone," Mr. Bagley said soothingly. "Even when you do expect it, it's difficult...even more so when you're caught off guard."

"I know, but I wanted—I wanted to—" She choked back a sob. "To just, at least, say good-bye."

Garret moved near to her and, wrapping his arms around her, he held her close. "Go ahead and cry," he said quietly. "You deserve a good cry, Megan."

"I just can't believe it," she sobbed. "I—I can't even say goodbye to him."

"You can still say goodbye," he said gently. "There are lots of ways to say goodbye."

"How?" She looked up at him through her tears.

"We'll go out in my boat. We'll go to the places on the river and the ocean that we know your father loved," he assured her. "We can even take his ashes out there sometime, if you want. I'm guessing that Rory would like that."

She sniffed. "Yeah, he probably would."

"We can go out whenever you want to, Megan. That's how you'll say goodbye."

"Yes, yes," Mr. Bagley said eagerly. "That's an excellent plan. And your father's urn will be ready to be picked up as soon as Tuesday morning. Or if you like, we can deliver it to the church in time for the service."

Megan nodded. "Yes, please do that. To the church. Thank you."

"Come on," Garret gently told her. "Let's go now."

Megan didn't protest as Garret led her out of the building. With one arm still wrapped around her shoulders, he led her down the street, away from the mortuary. And with each step he assured her that it was going to be okay. And that it was okay to cry.

Finally, they were standing in front of the newspaper office and she remembered their plan to look for the missing yellow envelope. "Thank you," she told Garret. "I don't know why I lost it in there."

"Seemed perfectly natural to me." He pushed a strand of windblown hair away from her face. "Especially when you consider everything, Megan. It's bad enough to lose your dad. But all this other business… Well, it's pretty trying."

"Yeah." She nodded as she opened her purse, digging in the bottom for the lure and key as well as her packet of tissues. Finding both, she blew her nose then unlocked the door. "I don't like feeling like such a basket case," she told him as they went inside. "I'm normally a little more together."

"I think you're pretty together already." He grinned at her. "Considering."

"Thanks." She was just turning on the lights when a recorded voice from the security system demanded she input the security code. "Oh, no," she said as she went over to the key pad. "I don't know the number."

"Michael was going to text it to your phone," Garret reminded her.

"My phone that's lost. Probably still in Dad's front yard."

Garret pulled out his phone, calling information to get the number of the security company just as the alarms started to go off.

"Let's go outside," she urged him.

It took a few minutes for her to convince the security company that she was Rory McCallister's daughter and, due to his death, the legal owner of the newspaper office. Even then they asked her some security questions, but finally they gave her the password to turn off the obnoxious alarm that was getting unwanted attention from passersby.

"And will you let the police know it's a false

alarm?" she asked. "I hate having them make an unnecessary trip." The truth was she didn't want to have to explain this to Detective Greene. "They have enough on their plate today."

"I have to let them know," the woman told her. "Whether they pay you a visit or not is up to them."

Megan rolled her eyes as she thanked the woman and hung up, handing Garret his phone back. "Well, it's good to know the system works. Too bad it wasn't working last night." She hurried inside and punched in the numbers which were, ironically, her birth date. She should've thought of that.

"I guess we can assume that no intruder has been here since last night," Garret said.

"Seems like it. And just to be safe, I think I'll reactivate the system so that no one sneaks in while we're here."

"Good idea."

Before long, they were in Rory's office. The police had given Megan permission to clean it up and put everything back together. "I should probably just box up all these files," she said as she laid a stack on top of his desk. "I'll have to eventually, anyway…when I sell it."

"So you really plan to sell the paper?"

"What else can I do?"

Garret shrugged. "Just seems a shame." He

worked to maneuver a file drawer back into the tall cabinet.

"A shame?"

He turned to look at her. "It's just that it's been in your family all these years. Rory was getting ready to celebrate the centennial next year. To think that the crooks have taken it all away from your family like this… Well, it just seems wrong, Megan."

She sighed as she wiped her dusty palms on her jeans. "I know."

"After all, you're a newspaper woman."

She pursed her lips then turned away, staring out the window, which was in need of a good washing. On the street people were still moving merrily along, dressed in vacation clothes and focused on their weekend activities, completely oblivious to the pain going on in her heart.

"I'm sorry," he said quickly. He came over to stand behind her, placing both hands on her shoulders. "I shouldn't have pushed you like that. You've already got so much to deal with." He turned her around to face him. "Please forgive me."

She tried to smile, but knew it was pathetic. "Of course."

"Can I give you a bit of advice, something that someone gave my grandmother after my grandfather passed?"

"What's that?"

"Don't make any major life decisions for at least three months. There's nothing, including this newspaper, that can't be put on hold for that long."

"Really?" She frowned. "I shouldn't just put the paper up for sale and get it over with?"

"I think you'd be wise to wait, Megan. You could end up regretting a knee-jerk decision, made in the wake of grief. Why not give yourself time?"

She nodded. "I guess that makes sense."

Garret looked around the dusty office. "I wonder if we're wasting our time in here, Megan. I mean, do you really think Rory would've hidden that envelope in his office? Seems like the first place somebody would look." He picked up another file drawer, sliding it into place.

"You're probably right."

"But it's possible that it's somewhere in the newspaper offices," Garret continued. "Can you think of any special spot where Rory might've put it?"

Megan tried to think. "There's no safe."

"Any quirky places that no one knew about?"

"Let's walk around," she suggested. "Maybe something will come to me." She turned off the lights in her dad's office and sadly closed the door. She could feel her dad's presence everywhere in this building. She knew that he'd had his hands all over anything that happened in here. A few employees, who never lasted long, had accused Rory McCallister of micromanaging this newspaper. And it was true—he did. But that was just who he was. It was one reason Megan hadn't ever felt she could work for him as an adult. But now that he was gone, she wished she'd given it a try.

"Are you okay?" Garret asked as they stood in the center of the press room.

She sighed. "Yeah…just thinking."

"Lots of good memories."

She swallowed against the lump in her throat. "Not enough. I wish we'd had time for more. Wish I could turn back the clock."

"Yeah, I get that. Same way I felt when my grandfather died." Garret went over to a dark corner, poking around.

"But in a way I can turn back the clock." She scanned the shelves on the back wall, wondering if the envelope might be tucked into one of those stacks of paper.

"How so?" he asked.

"By finishing what Dad started." She picked up an overturned bucket, looking inside it before she set it down again.

"You mean by bringing down the Marco brothers?" He looked a little uneasy, as if he didn't quite approve—or perhaps he was simply worried for her safety.

She just nodded then went over to kneel down to peer beneath one of the big machines, hoping to spy a yellow envelope. The more she looked, the more she realized that this could be like going back in time. If she could finish what Dad started with this exposé, it would be like she was working with him.

As she leaned over to see beneath a metal shelf, she said a silent prayer—partly to God and partly to her dad—asking for help to complete what seemed an impossible task. Then seeing an old yardstick, she used it to give a swipe beneath the shelf and hearing a loud snap, she jumped, letting out a little screech. But when she removed the yardstick, all she found was an old mousetrap latched on to the end of it. Well, at least she hadn't put her hand under there.

"Find something?" he asked as he came over to join her.

"No, but I'm not giving up," she said with fresh resolve. "I know in my heart that Dad would want me to finish this business. He obviously worked really hard on it. And I plan to—" She stopped at the sound of a door closing. "Did you hear that?" she whispered, grabbing onto his arm.

"Yeah." He nodded toward one of the big presses. "Let's get back there."

Together they went behind the greasy machine. "Do you think it's the police?" she asked quietly. "Remember the security company said they might come."

"They would've been here sooner."

"Yeah." She nodded, feeling that shaky feeling coming over her again as she remembered her attacker last night. But Garret was here now. She was safe with him.

"The alarm didn't go off," Garret pointed out. "Didn't you set it again?"

"I did." She frowned. "Maybe it's Barb or Arthur. They must know the code." She started to step out, but Garret stopped her.

"You wait here while I go make sure it's safe," he said in a commanding tone.

"But I'm sure that's who it is," she protested. "They simply disarmed the alarm. Let me go and talk to them."

"No." He firmly shook his head. "I'll go."

"But I—"

"Stay here," he told her as he stepped out.

She wanted to argue with him, to remind him that this was her newspaper office and that she was in charge, but he was already by the door. He turned off the light so that it was pitch-black in there and then he opened the door and slipped out into the office area.

She was tempted to follow him, but knew she'd never find her way out in the darkness without knocking something over and making noise that would alert an intruder to her whereabouts. But she really didn't think it was an intruder. She felt certain it was Barb or Arthur. And she felt like an indignant four-year-old who had been sent to her room.

As she stood there in the darkness with the inky, greasy smell of the press machines all around her, she began to question her blind trust in Garret. Oh, sure, he was handsome and kind and charming. But wasn't it a little suspicious that he seemed to know so much about the Marco brothers? Even more than the police seemed to know?

And why did he have so much interest in helping her? How was he able to so easily set his whole life aside while he stayed by her side? And why did it seem that every time something went awry, he was nearby? Sure, it seemed as if he was helping her. But how did he manage to come out of every encounter unscathed? Meanwhile, she'd been attacked and nearly killed. And then Michael had been shot.

A chill ran through her as she realized that Garret might simply be using her. What if she was the key for him to get his hands on that yellow envelope? Information that he needed to attain because he was working for the Marco brothers? What if he'd made up a story about being friends with her dad just to win her trust? And wasn't it fishy that he'd gone to so much trouble to keep her at his marina cabins? What if she'd been a stupid fool to fall for all this? Allowing a handsome face and a kind word to take her in? But here she was, stuck in a dark room—and she didn't even have a phone to call for help. Why hadn't she insisted he leave his phone behind? Why hadn't he offered?

Suddenly, she heard a scuffling sound in the main office. It sounded like chairs and desks being shoved around. This was followed by what seemed an exchange of words. And then a loud crash, as if something big had toppled over. And finally there was a single gunshot.

Her heart clutched in fear. Did Garret have his gun with him? She couldn't remember. What should she do? Stay put like Garret had told her? Or got out and risk being shot, too?

FOURTEEN

Megan's eyes had somewhat adjusted to the darkness, but she could still barely see as she fumbled along, trying to soundlessly feel her way to the door. At the same moment she realized that something was seriously wrong out there, and she immediately regretted her doubts about Garret. How could she have questioned him like that? She prayed as she shuffled through the dark room, feeling with her hands to keep from running into something. She prayed that Garret would be safe. Because she just knew—deep inside her—that he truly was her friend.

Finally, she felt the door, but now she was shaking so hard, she wasn't sure whether to open it or just stay put. The office was silent and she had no idea what was waiting on the other side of this door. She cracked it open. Seeing no one, she cautiously stepped out.

Nearby a desk and a couple of chairs were

overturned, blocking the aisle that led through the office. Still unsure if anyone was about, Megan crouched behind one of the desks that remained upright, trying to make her way to a desk phone so she could call for help. As she felt around the desktop, she remembered that her dad had finally agreed to cell phones for his reporters. Naturally, they no longer had landline phones on their desks. Only Barb's desk still had one.

Still crouched low, Megan inched her way to the front of the building, finally getting to Barb's desk where she remained tucked into the knee space, taking the phone down to her level to quietly dial 911. In a hushed voice, she gave her location and what little she knew. "There was a gunshot," she whispered. "And now it seems like I'm the only one in the building."

"Are you safe?"

"I don't know." Megan peeked above the top of the desk to see that the front door was open. "But it's Garret that I'm worried about."

"Can you move to a safer location?"

"I'm going to check on Garret." Megan dropped the phone and began to creep through the building. Garret could be wounded; he could need her help—she was tired of waiting!

Megan's search of the newspaper office revealed nothing, but she felt a wave of relief to see the flashing lights of the first police car. As it pulled in front of the newspaper office, she hurried outside. When Scott Barnett got out of the driver's side, she rushed over to talk to him, quickly explaining what had happened. "Garret might be hurt. I heard one gunshot, but I honestly can't remember if Garret had a gun on him or not."

Scott just nodded, talking into his radio and tipping his head to his partner, who was pulling on a bulletproof vest. Scott reached into the car for a vest for himself and then, as he put it on, he turned to Megan. "Get out of here," he ordered. "Go into Beulah's and stay there. We'll do what needs to be done here."

"Okay." She pressed her lips together, knowing she should do as he said, but the newspaper reporter in her wanted to stick around. Plus, she wanted to be nearby for Garret's sake. But when Scott scowled at her, she knew she needed to comply. She ran across the street to the restaurant, taking her post by the door.

"Something wrong at the newspaper office?" Jeanie, the waitress, asked as she paused with a tray of food to look out the window. "Another break-in? I was here last night when the cops came for that."

"Yeah." Megan sighed. "Another break-in. I just hope no one got hurt."

"Oh, dear, were the employees in there?"

"No. A friend of mine."

"Garret Larsson?" Jeanie asked.

Megan nodded. "Yes. How did you know that?"

"Oh, I noticed him outside of the place last night. With a young woman. Come to think of it, that must've been you."

"Yeah. That's right."

"And Garret was good friends with Rory. So it makes sense he'd be friends with you, too. Garret's a good guy." Jeanie tipped her head to Megan then continued with her tray, taking it to a booth by the window where the party, like most of the customers in the café, was watching Main Street with interest.

Megan appreciated Jeanie's endorsement of Garret. Except that it made her feel even more guilty for the way she had doubted him earlier. She knew her suspicions were partly due to being a journalist—and partly due to fear. But they were still wrong. Garret had not deserved that of her. She prayed silently again, begging God to take care of her dear friend—to keep him safe.

Another police car arrived, followed closely by an ambulance. Did that mean that someone inside had been hurt? Was it Garret? It took all her self-control to remain inside the café like

Scott had told her. But then, seeing that a crowd of curious spectators was gathering on this side of the street, she decided that she could probably blend in with them.

She cautiously stepped outside, looking up and down the street to be sure that no one suspicious was lurking about, getting ready to take a shot at her. But everything seemed normal out there. Well, except for the emergency vehicles. Although, to be fair, they were starting to seem fairly normal, too.

Please, God, she prayed silently, *let Garret be okay. Don't let him be hurt. If he is hurt, get help to him quickly.* As she prayed for him, she wondered what she would do without him. How would she ever manage to unravel this mess and find her dad's yellow envelope and expose the Marco brothers on her own? Furthermore, how would her heart handle it? Because Megan knew already she wanted Garret for more than just a good friend. Garret was the kind of man that she wanted to hold on to. Not just to help her out of this never-ending nightmare—but also to share in her dreams.

Slowing his jog to a fast walk, Garret rubbed his shoulder trying to determine which street his attacker had turned onto and wondering where the cops were. He was just about to reach for his phone when he heard a scuffling sound from the adjacent alley. Spinning around just in time to see a trash can being hurled at him, Garret dodged out of its path and then leaped toward his attacker.

The two crashed down to the asphalt, fists swinging as they rolled and fought. But the guy was quick and slippery. Garret finally had him by one arm and was just raising his gun to take aim. "Freeze right now!" Garret yelled. "Or I'll—" Before he could finish his sentence, he felt a sharp blow to his head and everything went dark.

When Garret came to, it was to the sound of sirens. Sitting up, he rubbed his head and, noticing red and blue lights flashing several blocks away, he remembered what had just happened. Suddenly, he remembered Megan and how he'd left her behind at the newspaper office. Seeing that the police cars and EMT truck were now parked there, blocking the traffic on Main Street, his heart began to pound even harder. Had something happened to Megan? It was obvious that Garret's attacker was not working alone—someone besides the man he'd been wrestling with had whacked him in the back of the head. What if they had gone back for Megan? Or perhaps they had another cohort who'd remained in the newspaper office after Garret had been lured into the chase. Despite his throbbing head, Garret began running, praying as he went—desperately hoping that Megan was not hurt.

As he got to the entrance of the newspaper office, he heard someone shouting his name. To his huge relief, it was Megan. Calling and waving, she burst out of a group of bystanders, rushing over to him.

"You're okay," she said with wide-eyed relief. "I was so worried."

He hugged her. "I'm fine. And you're okay, too?"

"Of course." She nodded.

"I felt bad to have left you alone like that," he confessed. "But I wanted to catch that guy."

"I was so worried for you." She looked into his eyes with such tenderness that he really wanted to kiss her. "I didn't know what to do."

He stroked her cheek. "I'm so glad you're all right." He wanted to kiss her, but the sound of yelling stopped him.

"There you are!" Scott Barnett exclaimed as he hurried over. Knowing that moment was gone, Garret explained what had just happened.

"No one else seems to be in the building," Scott told them. "But the officers are still looking around."

"I don't see how they got in." Megan told him about setting the alarm.

"You're sure it was on?" he said.

"I'm positive. The red light was flashing—showing it was activated."

"Let's go take a look," Scott said.

They went in to see that instead of the red light, it was the green light—showing it had been deactivated. "Someone had to punch in the code," she told Scott. "At the time I thought maybe it was an employee, but—"

"Which employees know the pass code?"

"Only Arthur and Barb as far as I know. But they obviously didn't break in here and attack Garret." She frowned. "But I just remembered something."

"What?" Scott asked.

"Michael called the security company last night. He promised to text me the pass code, which means it's probably in my phone."

Scott frowned. "Yeah?"

"I lost my phone at my dad's house this morning…I wonder if one of these guys found it."

"Sounds like you better change the pass code," Scott told them.

"And maybe I should get over to Dad's house and see if I can find my phone," she told him.

"How about if I follow you over there?" Scott offered. "The guys will be here for an hour or two, dusting for prints and gathering more evidence. Every piece we get helps to tighten the circle on these guys."

"Yeah." Megan gave a weary nod and Garret suspected she wasn't completely convinced of this. Who could blame her? So far it seemed that the bad guys were pretty much running the show.

Garret turned back to Scott. "We'd appreciate your backup."

Scott nodded. "I'll just let the guys know."

Garret slipped an arm around her, guiding her down Main Street, toward the funeral home where they'd left his SUV nearly two hours ago. After they got inside his vehicle, he handed his phone to her. "Go ahead and call the security company," he suggested. "Even if they didn't get your phone, they somehow figured out the code. Might as well change it now."

"Thanks."

As he drove, she placed the call. Garret kept a close eye on all the side streets just in case he spotted the jerk who'd jumped him.

Megan let out a long sigh after she hung up. "I need to talk to Detective Greene," she told Garret in an irritated tone.

"Was he at the newspaper office just now?" Garret asked.

"Not that I could see." She was digging a business card out of her purse. "Mind if I call him on your phone?"

"Not at all." Garret turned onto the beach road, driving slowly and keeping a close watch in his rearview mirror. Where was Scott?

"Detective Greene," Megan spoke slowly into the phone, almost as if she was bracing herself. "We need to talk." She listened for a moment then spoke more quickly. "Hang on a second." She turned to Garret. "I'm going to put it on speaker, okay?"

He just nodded. "But first tell him where we're headed and that we want backup ASAP. Tell him Scott was supposed to follow us, but I don't see him."

"Okay." Megan relayed this then pushed the button. "You're on speakerphone so Garret can hear you, too. Here's the deal. I want to know about my dad's autopsy."

"I can send you a copy of the report on the next business day." Greene's tone was crisp—all business. "After the holiday weekend, I'll have my assist—"

"I want to know about it *now*," Megan said firmly.

"What do you want to know?" The detective's tone suggested boredom. Garret could almost imagine him examining his nails with a blasé expression.

"I want to know what tests were actually run."

"I'm not sure what you're going after, Miss McCallister, but the coroner's report confirms that your father died of natural causes and—"

"How can you possibly *know* that?" she demanded.

"Because I read the coroner's report," he told her. "There were no wounds or signs of bruising or any indication of struggle or anything out of the ordinary."

"So what was the cause of death?" she asked.

"Drowning."

"Drowning?" She glanced at Garret. "He had on a life vest. And he was an excellent swimmer. How could he drown?"

"He was discovered facedown. Apparently, that's how he drowned."

"So you're suggesting my father's boat sank and he escaped without a scratch and then he simply ducked his head into the water and drowned? *Seriously?*"

"That was the coroner's finding."

"And the coroner—is he a medical examiner, or a trained physician—or is he just a city-appointed form-filler and paper-pusher?"

"Are you a concerned daughter or just a nosy reporter?"

"Both," she snapped back. "So let me just take a guess, Detective. The coroner *isn't* medically trained. He probably just rubber-stamped the report and—"

"I'm a busy man, Miss McCallister. Is there a real point to this *pleasant* little phone call or do you just make it your business to harass—"

"Yes, there's a point. I want you to explain to me how it's possible that your coroner could've gotten the results from the toxicology tests so quickly."

"Toxicology?" He blew out an exasperated sigh.

"Please, don't tell me you didn't request them."

"Why would your father need toxicology tests? From what I heard, he was a teetotaler. Or perhaps you suspect he had a drug problem, Miss McCallister."

Garret had to control himself now. What kind of an idiot was this detective? Besides being incredibly rude, he was just plain ignorant.

"First of all, he *was* a teetotaler. And I won't even respond to your other insinuation. But I would appreciate an answer, Detective Greene." Megan's tone grew more terse. "Did you request a toxicology report for my father or not?"

"Look," his voice softened slightly. "If I thought Rory McCallister was the sort of guy who would take anything—"

"I want you to understand me," she declared. "I am not suggesting my father intentionally ingested any intoxicating substance. But I would like to rule out the possibility that he was drugged by someone else. Can you grasp that?"

"Fine! I'll request toxicology."

"That would be impossible."

"Why?" he asked in a flat tone.

"My father was cremated today."

"Oh…?" There were a few seconds of silence. "And you authorized this?"

"No. I was totally blindsided by it." Megan proceeded to tell him of her dad's prearranged funeral plans. "I would've expected the coroner might've inquired about this before releasing the body to the mortuary."

"Well, it is a holiday weekend."

"So I keep hearing. But, as you can see, it's too late for toxicology now." Her voice had a catch in it, as if she was close to tears again. But something else was troubling Garret even more at the moment.

He slowed down on the beach road, preparing to turn onto her dad's road, but the whole while keeping his eyes on a dark sedan that was parked on the side of the road about half a mile beyond them. "Megan," he said urgently.

"What?" She turned from the phone.

"Look." He tipped his head toward the sedan. "I think I've seen that car before."

She narrowed her eyes at the car then turned

back to the phone. "Look, Detective Greene," she said urgently. "You messed up on the toxicology reports, but something else is up. We're just about to my dad's house and there's a suspicious-looking vehicle down the road. Garret thinks it belongs to the—"

"You need to send a couple of patrol cars out here immediately," Garret yelled into the phone. He turned onto Rory's road then stopped. "I'm sure it's the same sedan I saw last night. You guys better move fast."

"And you should get out of there," Detective Greene said quickly. "We'll be there ASAP. You stay on the line."

"You better hurry!" As Garret backed up, getting onto the main beach road, he could see the sedan starting to slowly move toward them. "We're heading back toward town," he shouted into the phone.

Megan turned to look through the back window. "They're following us. Speeding up, too," she yelled into the phone. "Definitely pursuing us."

"Scott's just confirmed he's on the way and I'm requesting additional backup," the detective assured them. "I'm coming, too."

"Hurry," Garret said. "They're in hot pursuit and for all we know they're armed!" He pressed the accelerator, pushing it to sixty on the slightly bumpy road. "Get down!" he warned Megan as the speedometer passed seventy, moving toward eighty. As they flew down the nearly deserted beach road, he silently prayed that the thugs behind them weren't armed—and that he could keep his vehicle from bouncing off this washboard section of road.

"Hold on!" he yelled at Megan. He braked suddenly, jerking the SUV onto a sandy strip of road that led straight to the beach. Putting the SUV into four-wheel drive, he pushed it as fast as he could, hoping the low sedan would follow and get stuck in the loose sand. That was, unless he got stuck first. As his tires churned and ground into the sand, he knew that was a real possibility.

FIFTEEN

Megan tried to brace herself as the SUV bounced along the rutted surface and onto the dune. Despite Garret's warning to stay down, she lifted her head just high enough to see the steep dune looming before them. Could this SUV handle the steep grade, or would they end up tumbling over on the beach?

She turned to peer over the seat and out the rear window to see that the dark car was still in pursuit and not far behind them. Surely they couldn't make it down the dune without ruining their car. Or maybe they didn't care.

"Hang on!" Garret yelled as the SUV started down the dune.

With wide eyes, Megan watched and prayed. And to her relief, the SUV remained upright and they were soon on the beach. She looked back through the rear window to see that the car had stopped.

"They're either stuck or they've given up," she announced.

Garret kept driving, going far enough down the beach so that they were out of sight from the portion of bluff where they'd gotten away from the car.

"Looks like the coast is clear," Garret said as he stopped the SUV. "Well, not literally."

Megan glanced nervously around, feeling slightly relieved to see tourists here and there along the beach.

"I hope that car is stuck." Garret kept a close lookout behind them.

"And then the police can pick them up."

"I think I hear sirens." Garret put his window down and she could faintly hear them, too.

Megan suddenly remembered the phone in her hand. "Detective Greene?" she asked tentatively.

"Yeah?" he answered gruffly.

She quickly explained their location and Garret asked if any of the cops had spotted the sedan yet.

"Not that I've heard. We're almost to Rawlins Road now. You stay there on the beach," Detective Greene told them. "We'll let you know how it goes down, but I need to hang up."

"We'll be here," Garret said into the phone.

Megan hung up. "He actually sounded somewhat involved and concerned."

"Nice for a change."

With the sounds of sirens getting closer, Megan looked at the carefree vacationers out enjoying the good weather on the beach. Although a few looked around with interest at the sound of the police sirens, most seemed completely oblivious to the dangers nearby. It was reassuring to see normal people acting like normal people. Like maybe the whole world hadn't gone crazy, after all.

Megan let out a weary sigh as she gazed out toward the churning waves. With all the happenings these past couple days, she hadn't even taken a moment to enjoy the seascape that she usually loved to soak in while visiting here. "Looks like a fog bank on the horizon." She nodded toward the ocean.

"Yeah, I heard the weather's supposed to turn cool by tomorrow. Might put a damper on the Memorial Day parade." He was heading the SUV slowly down the beach, stopping on a less crowded stretch of sand. "We'll do like Detective Greenhorn says and just stay put awhile." He glanced up and down the beach with a watchful expression.

Megan waved a teasing finger at him. "You do know it's illegal to drive a motor vehicle on the beach, don't you?"

He gave a half smile. "I think the police will give us a pass today."

Megan leaned back in the comfortable leather seat in an attempt to relax. "I feel like I'm stuck in some weird action movie," she said quietly, "or maybe it's a video game. It seems like no matter what we do or where we go, someone is trying to kill us."

"I know. I was just thinking the same thing. Nowhere feels safe." He tipped his head toward his side window, looking up toward the bluff. "If someone was up there with a high-powered rifle, we could be in trouble right now."

She jerked to attention, looking past him to see what he was pointing at. "Can you see anyone?"

"No. Just saying."

She leaned back again, taking in a deep calming breath.

"You know, Megan, if they really wanted us dead, they've had their opportunities," Garret said slowly.

"Meaning?" She glanced over at him.

"Meaning, they might be keeping us alive in the hopes that we'll find that envelope for them. And then they'll probably knock us off."

"But what about my attacker last night?" she questioned. "He was ready to kill me."

"I'm sure it seemed that way, but maybe he just wanted to scare information out of you."

She considered this. "Well, if I'd had information, it probably would've worked. I was pretty scared."

"I'm starting to think they just want to make us understand that they're playing hardball."

"How many of these thugs do you think there might be?"

"Good question. Offhand, I'd guess they might have at least five guys. Between the boat, the guys in the car, the guys we've seen on foot—well, it's hard to say, but it's no small-time operation."

"And if they're working for the Marco brothers like Dad suspected, and if the Marco brothers really are involved in organized crime, I'm sure they'd have more than just a couple of guys."

"I wish Rory had told me more of the details about what all was in that envelope."

She sighed. "I wish I knew where he'd hidden it. Or that he'd simply handed it over to the police."

"I'm sure that was his plan—after the release of his story to the public. Rory told me he wanted to run it in the newspaper so that everyone in town would know what was going on—all at the same time. He'd even talked about getting other media sources here. He wanted to make it into a big deal so that Cape Perpetua citizens would be willing to do something about it. And it won't be easy to deal with the Marcos. Not without everyone behind it. I seriously doubt that the local police can handle it alone."

"That makes sense. Especially considering how a lot of the locals, including some of the police force, feel like the casino and the restaurant have really pumped life back into this town."

"Well, in a way they have. Money does that."

"Even when it's illegally gained money."

"Unfortunately."

Megan studied Garret's profile and was struck, once again, by how handsome he was. "I'm curious about something," she said suddenly.

"What?" He turned to look at her.

"Oh—nothing." She waved her hand and turned away in embarrassment. What had she almost done? "Never mind."

"Okay, now I really want to know," he told her. "Nothing gets my curiosity up as much as someone starting to say something then putting on the brakes. What are you curious about, Megan?"

"Forget it. Sorry, it was silly."

"Come on." He reached over, giving a playful tug on the sleeve of her denim jacket. "Out with it."

"Okay." She turned back to look at him, knowing her slip up was probably a result of exhaustion and stress. "I was just curious as to why someone like you— I mean, you seem like a pretty great guy—at least as far as I can tell. Anyway, why hasn't some smart woman snatched you up by now?"

He threw back his head and laughed. "Well, thank you. I'll take that as a compliment, Megan."

She frowned at him. "It was meant to be a question. And since you forced it out of me, I must insist that you answer it."

"I'm guessing you're pretty good at grilling people," he teased.

"Inquiring minds want to know." She folded her arms in front of her, waiting.

"Well, I won't try to pretend I've never had a girlfriend." He chuckled. "But the truth is there haven't been many. As you might remember, I was pretty shy in high school. Going through my parents' marital problems in the public eye... well, it wasn't easy."

Megan vaguely remembered the scandal involving his mom and the junior high principal— and something about his dad had gone through the rumor mill, too, but she honestly couldn't recall the details. "I can sort of relate," she told him. "When my parents got divorced, it seemed like it was everyone's business. Your family stuff probably felt similar."

"Only it was even more public."

"Maybe, but I get the sense you are skirting my question," she said in a journalistic tone.

He nodded. "Well, anyway, my first real girlfriend dumped me in college. Well, *girlfriend* is probably an overstatement since she only went out with me a few times. But as it turned out I was more into her than she was into me. I suppose that hurt my pride some."

"That's understandable."

"I had a couple more relationships after that. But nothing very serious. At least not on my end. And then I got busy working at the marina after my grandpa passed away. I really haven't had time to pursue any kind of serious romance."

"I'm sure that some women might've tried to pursue you." She gave him a sly look.

"Maybe so. But no one that I was interested in." He gazed at her with what felt like more than just a casual glance, making her cheeks grow warm. "So now that I told you about my lackluster dating history, how about you tell me about yours."

She shrugged. "There's not much to tell. Strangely enough, it would sound very similar to yours. So much so you might think I made it up."

"Really?" He brightened like this was good news.

"I had one semiserious relationship. Also in

college. We dated for nearly a year before he dumped me."

Garret frowned. "I don't know why anyone would dump you. The guy must've been an idiot."

She smiled. "Thanks."

His eyes lit up. "But I'm selfishly glad that he did."

"You are?" She blinked in pleasant surprise.

"Uh-huh." He grinned as he placed his hand on her shoulder. "Girls like you don't happen along every day."

Just then his phone began to ring and, realizing she still had it in her hand, she gave it back to him and because he put it on speaker mode, she could hear him talking to Scott Barnett.

"I don't know how we missed the car," Scott told him. "We had cruisers on both ends of the beach road. And last we heard they were supposedly headed north, right?"

"That was my guess. They obviously wouldn't go south since that road is impassable down there." Garret explained about how he'd departed the road for the beach. "By the time I heard sirens, I would've estimated the sedan would've been coming to the intersection to town."

"Well, somehow we missed him." Scott asked where they were and Garret explained. "We'd still like to go up to Rory's place and look around."

"I'll meet you there," Scott told him. "From here on out, until we catch these guys, we don't plan to let you and Megan out of our sight."

"Great." Garret turned on his engine. "We appreciate it."

After he said goodbye, Garret aimed the SUV back to the sandy access road. "You still need to look for your phone," he reminded her. "And we really need to find your dad's big yellow envelope."

"But didn't you insinuate that if we find it, they won't have any reason not to kill us?"

"Well, it's not as if we'll advertise that we found it."

"That's true." Megan suddenly got an idea. "Unless we did just that."

"Huh?" Garret was cautiously looking both ways on the quiet beach road, before entering it.

"I have an idea."

"Okay, let's hear it." He turned right, heading toward her dad's house.

"What if we made a fake envelope?"

"A fake envelope?"

"Kind of like bait," she continued. "We could go someplace where we know we'd be seen by one of the bad guys, and we could pretend to exchange it."

"And then get killed?" he asked.

"Hopefully not. We'd need the police all around. Probably undercover, though, since the whole point would be to draw the bad guys out—at least some of them. If the police could get them in custody they could question them. Maybe some of them would talk."

Garret slowly nodded. "You know, that kind of makes sense." He pointed to where Scott was just pulling into Rory's driveway.

"Well, unless we find the real envelope," she added. "In that case, we just get it into the hands of the police and let them take care of it."

"Hopefully, we'll find it." Garret pulled up behind Scott's police car. "At least we'll give it our best try."

They exchanged hasty greetings with the police, but Scott and his partner Derrick Freeman insisted on going inside ahead of them. "I don't see any sign of intruders, but keep a safe distance behind us," Scott told them as Megan handed over the key.

To her surprise, Garret took her hand, keeping her close to him in a comfortingly protective way as they followed the cops up to the house.

"Stay right there." Scott pointed to a screened corner by the porch. "Until we are sure it's unoccupied."

Megan watched as both cops drew their guns

and, calling out, let themselves into the house. "I really don't think there's anyone inside, but I'm glad we didn't come alone," she whispered as she and Garret hovered in the corner by the porch.

"At this point nothing would surprise me." Garret was keeping a close watch all around them. "These guys are really driven, Megan. My guess is that they've been offered a big chunk of cash to deliver the goods."

"That's why my decoy envelope makes sense," she said quietly.

"Except for the danger factor." He pulled her closer to him, wrapping his left arm around her shoulders, but keeping his right hand free and near his gun holster.

"You guys can come in," Scott called out after several minutes. "Doesn't look like anyone has been here since the last break-in."

"I want to look for my phone first," Megan told them. "It should be right around here."

Garret pulled out his own phone. "I'll call your number and we can listen for the ring."

"Good idea." She studied the grassy area near the porch as he hit the speed dial.

"It's ringing," he said.

"I can't hear it." She strained her ears as she poked around in the tall grass. It was in need of mowing. Something her dad liked to do on Saturdays...like today.

"It only rang twice then stopped." Garret turned to her. "Like someone answered and then hung up."

"So they have my phone." Megan let out a long sigh as she stood up straight. "Everything is in that phone, too. I can't believe I was so careless."

"People tend to get careless when running for their lives." He reached over to pat her shoulder. "Don't worry, we'll get it back somehow."

Although she doubted this, she nodded, bracing herself as Garret opened the front door. Was she ready to go in there—to see what those creeps had done to Dad's house?

SIXTEEN

Despite Scott's reassurance that the house was empty, Megan still felt uneasy as she and Garret worked their way through the rooms and closets. They had decided to work as teams. Scott and his buddy working upstairs, she and Garret down below.

Together they searched the living room and kitchen and laundry room. All to no avail. Eventually, they found themselves standing in the center of the attached garage. It, too, had been turned upside down.

"What a mess." Garret shook his head.

"Oh, look at that," Megan said with disgust. "They even went through Dad's chest freezer." She knelt down to gather up some frozen packages still on the floor, putting them back into the old appliance. Fortunately, they still felt fairly firm. "Hopefully, they're okay." She tossed what looked like a whole salmon back into the deep freeze, sad to think how her dad had probably been looking forward to putting this on his barbecue grill this summer.

"I can't believe they bothered with the freezer," Garret said. "Or maybe they're just a bunch of vandals."

"I'm not sure they know it or not, but it actually makes sense they looked in here." Megan bent over to rearrange the paper-wrapped packages.

"How's that?" Garret knelt down to pick up a few bundles, loading them into his arms.

"When I was a girl, Dad was working on a suspense novel. As usual, he wrote it on his typewriter. And he hadn't made a copy. So when we were gone for a few days, he put his manuscript in the freezer."

"What for?"

"His theory was that if the house burned down, his manuscript would survive in the freezer." She continued looking at each package, hoping to discover the yellow envelope tucked amidst them.

Garret chuckled. "Makes sense." He read the names of the contents as he handed her the packages. "Steelhead. Halibut. Coho. Bait." He chuckled. "Reminds me of your idea for trapping the crooks."

"Yeah, it's kind of a fisherman idea, isn't it?"

"The more I think about it, the more I think we should keep it in mind."

"Me, too."

They left the garage and reentered the house. Garret and Megan made good progress putting the place together, but no progress in locating the yellow envelope. Scott and Derrick weren't faring any better, and they'd even searched things like the toilets' water tanks, behind the fireplace's closed flue and some other interesting places.

While Garret and Megan were going through her dad's office one last time, Megan pulled out a bundle of yellow envelopes. "I'm guessing Dad probably used one of these." She waved them at Garret.

"Yep." Garret nodded.

Megan removed an envelope then began to stuff it with a couple of fishing magazines and a folded up old newspaper. She fastened it closed, roughed it up a bit then held it up. "How's this look?"

Garret came over to examine her handiwork. "Not bad. But the original one had some writing on it."

"Do you remember what it said?"

He frowned. "The name of the reservation and the date and then his name. And it might've said *investigation* or *evidence* or something. Because I remember looking at it and immediately feeling intrigued."

"Was the writing just on the envelope? Or a label?"

"It was written right on the envelope in black felt pen. Not in the center, though. More in this corner." He pointed to the left-hand upper portion. "Fairly big lettering, though. Like he wanted it to be easy to read." He held up his fingers to show her. "Neat penmanship, too."

"Yes. Dad had very neat penmanship." She dug around his desk to find a black Sharpie. "He took some drafting in college and liked to write like an architect. I'm pretty good at imitating it." She leaned down, writing the reservation's name on top then a date from last week beneath it as well as her dad's name. Finally, she wrote Investigative Evidence beneath it. "How's this?"

Garret blinked. "That looks strikingly similar."

"Think anyone would fall for it?"

"Hey." Scott's eyes lit up when he came into the room to see her holding the envelope up. "You found it?"

Megan explained her faux envelope. "I thought if we exchanged it in a public place—sort of like bait—with some undercover cops around…well, we might just catch ourselves a fish."

"Or a rat," Garret added. "Hopefully, several rats."

"Interesting idea." Scott frowned slightly.

"But I'm not sure you should be involved in baiting anyone connected to the mob. It could be dangerous for Megan."

"More dangerous than being randomly mugged or shot at?" Megan asked him.

"Good point." Scott picked up the thick envelope, studying it more closely. "I just wish this was the real thing. That would help a lot."

"Well, I haven't given up yet," Megan assured him. "No stone unturned, right?"

"Right," Garret agreed.

It was after six when they finally finished searching and straightening the house, and now she and Garret were standing in the front yard discussing the case with Scott and Derrick. To Megan's relief both cops seemed determined to resolve it. Mostly because they were upset over fellow cop Michael Conrad being shot.

"At least his surgery went well," Scott told them. "I talked to Mrs. Conrad a little while ago and he's in really good spirits."

"I plan to visit him in the morning," Garret said.

"Me, too," Megan agreed. "But right now I'm starving. Hey, I have an idea. Let's all go to Marco's."

Garret's brows arched. "Marco's? Are you serious, Megan?"

"Yeah, I'm craving Italian."

"Is this about food or are you planning to go fishing?" Scott's dark eyes twinkled with interest.

"Fishing?" Derrick looked confused.

Megan patted her oversize bag, where the envelope was safely zipped inside. "The bait's right here."

Garret quickly explained her plan to Derrick. "But we need someone to hand it off to," he said to Scott. "And we need to make it look like we're being tricky. Can't be obvious, you know?"

"Well, Derrick and I have finished our shift," Scott said. "But I suppose we could get into plain clothes and give you some assistance with it. I wouldn't mind."

"Yeah," Derrick eagerly agreed. "I'm down with that."

"But I'll have to get approval from Detective Greene," Scott said as he reached for his phone. "Want me to ask?"

"Yes." Megan nodded with enthusiasm. And they all waited for Scott to explain the fishing plan to Detective Greene. To everyone's relief, Greene liked the idea and asked to be put on speakerphone. For several minutes he acted like he was in charge, and they all cooperated with him to concoct a basic plan.

Garret and Megan would appear to be going to dinner, but they would make the yellow envelope visible—not obvious, but tempting. Just like bait. The two officers, in their plain clothes, would show up about a half hour later, positioning themselves in the lounge as if to have drinks, but where they could keep an eye on things. The two parties would stay in touch via texting and if no one had tried to snag the envelope by the time Megan and Garret were having their dessert and coffee, the policemen—who would be recognizable due to the small town—would show up at their table and take the envelope from them in a visible way—a way to convince the crooks that it was too late.

"What if no one in the mob is around to see it?" Scott asked.

"That would be unusual," Garret told them. "Every time I've gone there, I've seen at least one of the Marcos hanging around. Maybe not working, but they are there. It's a family business, after all."

"But what if they don't take the bait?" Derrick asked. "What good will it do to just pass a fake envelope around?"

"At the least, it should get the mob off Megan's back," Garret declared. "What would be the point if they think the police have the evidence?"

"That's right," Greene agreed. "Make sure you guys have concealed weapons on you."

"I'll be armed, too," Garret told them.

* * *

As Garret drove them into town, Megan looked down at her denim jacket and jeans. "I hope I'm not too grubby for Marco's," she said with concern.

"Remember where you are," Garret told her. "This is Cape Perpetua, not Seattle. It's pretty casual here. And the tourists sure don't dress for dinner."

"Yeah, you're probably right."

"I just hope we can get a table." Garret tapped the clock on the dashboard. "It's dinnertime on a Saturday night."

"Oh, yeah—and a holiday weekend, too." She frowned. "And I was really starting to crave Italian."

"I was craving an end to all this madness."

By the time they reached the restaurant, it was seven. And Marco's was crowded—with a waiting list and numerous parties already ahead of them. Garret gave the hostess his name then tossed an uneasy glance at Megan.

"It'll be at least thirty, maybe forty minutes," the hostess informed them. "But you might find room to wait in the lounge."

"Hey…" Garret's tone grew intimate as he leaned toward her like they were old friends. "How about getting us a table on the deck?" He nodded toward the windows that overlooked the river. A couple groups of diners were out there. "That doesn't look too busy."

"We're supposed to stop seating out there at seven. It's getting chilly."

Garret's smile warmed. "But it's barely past seven now. I'm sure you could sneak us out there if you really wanted to. You look like a girl with clout."

Her dark eyes twinkled. "Well, okay. You'll be the last ones out there tonight. But you better promise me you won't complain if it gets cold."

"You won't hear a peep out of us," he assured her. "Thanks."

The hostess tossed an interested look at Megan as she led them outside. Perhaps she wondered what their relationship was, if Garret was available. She led them to a table for two. Next to the railing, it overlooked the river and bridge, with a stainless-steel propane heater right next to it. The hostess laid down two oversize leather-covered menus and then turned on the propane heater. "Here you go."

"This is lovely," Megan told the hostess as she sat down. "If it wasn't foggy, we could probably see the sunset from here." After the hostess left, Megan started to question herself. Was it really a good idea to be here tonight? Wasn't it a little like dining in the lion's den?

"Are you okay?" Garret had what seemed a forced smile.

"Just wondering if this was a smart move." She glanced around uneasily.

"I actually think it was. Honestly, I can't imagine the Marcos doing anything crazy on their own property. Not with all their valued customers around to witness it."

She slowly nodded. "I guess that makes sense. They wouldn't want to mess this pretty place up." She glanced around the impressive deck. From its marble-topped teak tables and comfortable padded teak chairs to the attractive potted plants and trees set prettily about, and then the stone fireplace that the two other groups of diners were seated near, it all looked lovely—and expensive. "This place is really uptown for little old Cape Perpetua," she observed.

"And this is the *casual* part of the restaurant," he told her.

"I can see why Dad got suspicious of the Marcos. Restaurants in this town usually struggle to stay afloat. It really does look like they were skimming from the tribe. I'm surprised others weren't suspicious."

He nodded. "Yeah, it's kind of in-your-face opulence. There was some talk at first, but eventually people got used to it. A lot of locals are proud to have such a fancy waterfront restaurant."

"I'm guessing it's been hard on the Bridgeview."

"That's an understatement. I was talking to Marty Stephens last week. If they don't start doing better this season, he said he'll be shut down by winter."

"That's so sad. Bridgeview was where Dad always took me for special occasions—birthdays, graduation, holidays. I have happy memories there."

"You and most everyone else in town…although they seem to have forgotten them."

"Well, I'd feel more comfortable at Bridgeview than—" She stopped talking as a young man brought them their hot drinks. But as he set the cups and saucers on the table, he suddenly jerked—as if something had startled him—slopping a bit of Garret's coffee onto the marble.

"Sorry," he said quickly, using Garret's linen napkin to blot the spill before he quickly hurried away, leaving the soiled napkin splayed on the table.

"Kind of a rude waiter," Megan said. "I'm surprised they—"

"There was a reason for that." Garret used an even tone, keeping a pleasant expression as he picked up his cup.

"What?"

"That man was my employee. Kent Jones. I hired him as a mechanic a couple weeks ago.

To be honest, his mechanic work was no better than his waiting skills. But then he disappeared." He narrowed his eyes slightly. "And now he's working here."

"Sounds like you're better off without him." She picked up her menu, perusing the tempting entrées.

"That's true."

"So do you think he was embarrassed to see you?" She laid down her menu.

"I think it's more than that. But maybe having him here will help our fishing plan. In fact, I'm guessing he's talking to one of the Marcos right now. Informing someone that we're out here."

Megan glanced nervously at her bag, still right where she'd put it under the table, next to her feet. The yellow envelope was still barely sticking out, but visible for anyone looking for it. She'd removed her personal items from the bag—in case someone nabbed it—dumping everything into Garret's glove box for safekeeping.

"But we need to play it cool." Garret took a casual sip of coffee.

"Yes." She selected a tea bag from the little basket, trying to look at ease as she opened it and dropped it into the black porcelain teapot.

"But I hope you weren't too set on Italian food."

"Why?" Her stomach rumbled hungrily.

"Well, I don't know about you, but I'm not comfortable eating food fixed by anyone associated with the Marco brothers."

She cringed inwardly as she lowered her voice. "You think they might poison us?"

"Probably not. But I'm still not comfortable with it." His eyes moved over her shoulder. "Here comes our waiter now."

"Do you know him?" she said quietly.

He shook his head, then sipped his coffee. "Just act natural as you order."

"Okay."

The waiter came and, without any incident, politely took their orders and left. Once again, Megan questioned the sensibility of this plan. And yet, if it worked, it could be very helpful. But as waiters came and went, Megan began to doubt her plan completely.

"So…Kent is up to something," Garret said quietly, keeping a congenial expression on his face.

"Uh-huh?" Megan tried to act natural.

"Act nonchalant while I keep an eye on things." He took another sip of coffee. "The waiter he's speaking to looks suspicious. And don't look now, but he's coming our way."

Megan forced a smile as a slim guy carrying a water pitcher came to their table. He greeted them, acting like they were his good friends.

Then leaning over to fill Megan's water glass, he let the pitcher slip, dumping the contents into her lap. In one swift move, he grabbed up her bag and was about to bolt when Garret clasped his arm. "Let it go!" he growled as he pinned the waiter against the railing.

As the waiter struggled to get away from Garret's grasp, Megan snagged the heavy glass water pitcher. Giving it a hard swing, she used it to whack him in the back of the head. The waiter went down and, in the same instant, Garret snatched the bag and envelope with such force that he lost his balance and fell back. Before Megan could get to him, Garret toppled backward over the top of the railing, plummeting downward to what had to be a twenty-foot drop below.

SEVENTEEN

Megan ran to peer over the railing, seeing nothing but dark gleaming water below, but at least the tide was in. The water would've helped break his fall—if it was deep enough. Megan dashed past the waiter who was on the deck still rubbing his head. Running by startled customers, she prayed that Garret was okay.

She exited the building and sprinted to the lower deck, across a gangway, and down to the dock below. She had to get to him, fast. A bad fall like that could have broken his neck...he could be drowning. Tragic thoughts ran through her mind. Where were Scott and Derrick?

When Megan finally got down by the piers that supported the restaurant, she could hear voices. "Garret?" she yelled.

"He's over here," a male voice shouted back.

"Who's that?" she demanded.

"Officer Freeman," he yelled back. "Derrick."

"I'm coming," she shouted as she began climbing and tripping over the riffraff rocks. Getting her feet wet, she stumbled toward the officer and found him standing beside Garret. "Are you okay?"

"I'm fine," Garret called back. "Just wet."

Relief flooded her as she joined them. "I was so worried." She hugged him, getting herself wet as she did so. "You're soaking."

"Yeah. Falling into the river does that."

"You're sure you're okay?"

"Yeah, but let's get out of here."

It wasn't long until the three of them were standing in the parking lot where Garret removed a blanket from his SUV and wrapped it around himself like a cape. "What's going on up there?" Garret asked Derrick, who was checking something on his phone.

"Scott and Detective Greene got the guy who wrestled you for the envelope," Derrick said as he put his phone back into the shoulder strap.

"So the fishing plan worked?" Megan said in wonder.

"We need to get you guys out of here," Derrick suggested. "Scott doesn't want you to go back into the restaurant."

"Not like this, anyway." Garret shivered.

"Yeah, you need to get dried off," Megan told him.

"Will you be at the marina?" Derrick asked.

"Yeah." Garret nodded. "No place else to go."

"I'll ask Detective Greene to assign someone to keep watch over there for the rest of the night." Derrick talked on his phone as he escorted them across the parking lot. By the time they reached Garret's SUV, it was all set. "Officers Reynolds and Harter are on their way to the marina," he told them as they got into the vehicle.

Garret started the engine, turning up the heat as he headed out of the parking lot. "Well, that was unexpected."

"You could've been killed." Once again, Megan wondered what she'd do without him. Not just because of the dilemma they both seemed to be trapped in...but because of something more. Garret was unlike anyone she'd ever known. The previous guys in her life had never made her feel like this. Not just the attraction, either—although it was very real—but Garret made her feel secure. Despite knowing she was still in danger, she felt protected.

"I'm just glad it wasn't low tide." He shook his head.

Megan shuddered to think of Garret crashing headfirst onto the rocks that jutted out of the water at low tide.

"But God's watching out for us, Megan. I believe it."

"I do, too."

"And it was a small price to pay to catch a thug or two."

"Well, that's a pretty good victory," she declared. "I'm glad they went for the bait."

"And when Tony and Vince find out, it'll sure give them something to think about. I'm guessing they'll want to back off if they think the police have that envelope. So, yeah, I think we're safer. Just the same, I'm still relieved to know the police will send someone to watch the marina."

"I wish it was the real envelope." Megan sighed. "I won't feel really safe until the whole Marco gang is rounded up. Although I do feel safer when I'm with you, Garret. I was so scared when you went over the railing. I don't know what I'd do if you'd really been hurt...or worse."

He reached over to give her hand a squeeze. "Good thing I'm a tough nut, huh?"

"Even a tough nut can crack." She wrapped her fingers around his cold ones, trying to share some warmth. "Seriously, Garret, I don't want to lose you."

He tightened his grasp on her hand. "I don't want to lose you either, Megan. I'm determined not to."

She felt a surge of happiness—Garret was as much into her as she was into him. Now if only they could find the missing envelope and help the police put away the criminals.

As soon as they got back to the marina, Megan felt relieved to realize she wouldn't be staying alone in the little cabin again tonight. Despite how Garret had fixed it up, she didn't like the idea of being by herself.

Garret unlocked the door to his house to the sound of Rocky's barking. But it was reassuring to know the dog was keeping watch. He led Megan inside. "My apologies for my bachelor housekeeping," he said as he closed and locked the door. "I think you should stay in the master suite. It's the most secure part of the house."

"I don't want to put you out of your room, Garret."

"You won't be. I still use the same room I've had since I was a kid." He grinned as he patted Rocky. "Until that master suite gets redecorated, which hasn't made the top of my priority list yet, I'm in no hurry to use it." He shivered with the now-damp blanket still over his shoulders.

"Okay. Well, if it's not putting you out, I accept." She pointed to his soggy clothes. "But you need to get dried off and warmed up."

He pointed back at her. "You look damp, too. Make yourself at home." He nodded to her bags in the living room then pointed to a nearby door. "The master suite."

She thanked him then gathered her things and opened the door to the mysterious master suite. But she immediately understood why Garret wasn't eager to stay there. Everything in the spacious room was Victorian, with purple and pink cabbage roses and lace abounding. China knickknacks were everywhere, coated with dust. But Megan knew she wouldn't complain as she set her bags on the flowery quilt of the king-size bed. She was grateful for a safe haven, even if it did look like a granny room.

And when she saw the dead bolt on the solid bathroom door, she understood why Garret had described the suite as safe. With the heavy door and no window, this bathroom would not be easily broken into.

She changed out of her damp clothes, due to the hug of relief she'd shared with Garret, then went back into the living room. Still hungry, she decided to take him up on his invitation to make herself at home. And going directly to the kitchen, she started to poke around. Before long she discovered packaged lasagna in the freezer, which she immediately put in the oven, as well as enough ingredients to make a green salad. And since the lasagna was going to take a while, she opened some tomato basil soup and it was fragrantly steaming on the stove by the time Garret joined her. With damp hair and fresh clothing, he looked so handsome that she had to divert her eyes to keep from staring.

"Something smells good." Garret pulled out a stool to sit at the breakfast bar.

"You told me to make myself at home." She tossed the last of the chopped cucumber into the greens. "And I must say, for a guy, you keep a pretty well-stocked fridge and pantry. I'm impressed."

He chuckled. "It's just the result of frugality. Saves money to eat at home—and time, too."

She smiled. "I like that."

Garret woke up early on Sunday morning. Partly because, exhausted after a long day, they'd both turned in early the night before. But as he showered and shaved, he couldn't stop thinking about Megan. Their quiet dinner and easy conversation had felt so comfortable and natural last night. Not only like a much-needed respite, but as if they had a real connection, like they'd been friends for years...as if they could easily become something more. It had taken all his willpower not to kiss her good-night. And that was simply because he didn't want to rush things. Megan had been on an emotional roller coaster these past few days. He instinctively knew that stepping into a romantic relationship could backfire on him. And due to his strong feelings toward Megan, he wasn't sure he wanted to risk pushing her too far too quickly. What if she thought he was taking unfair advantage of her vulnerable situation? Besides, she had just lost her dad.

As he dressed, her felt relieved that no more drama had interrupted a night of good rest. Having a manned patrol car parked in front of the marina, plus Rocky's bed near the front door, had been reassuring. And he hoped the worst of this drama was behind him. However, one thing was seriously troubling him. That was seeing Kent at Marco's on the Waterfront last night. And his involvement with that other waiter. Very suspicious.

"Good morning," Megan said cheerfully as Garret came into the kitchen. "I hope you don't mind that I started a pot of coffee."

"Not at all. Thank you. I wasn't sure you were up. Couldn't blame you for sleeping in. I'm sure you were exhausted."

"I slept so well that I was ready to get up." She grinned as she poured a cup of coffee. "That Victorian boudoir is more comfortable than it looks."

He chuckled. "Well, my grandma sure loved it." He went over to the fridge, opening it to see what he might fix them for breakfast. "I think it's my turn to cook this morning. I thought I'd make something simpler than yesterday. Eggs and toast okay with you?"

"Sounds perfect." She took her coffee to the breakfast bar, watching and visiting as he cooked.

"I woke up thinking about my ex-employee Kent Jones."

"The waiter at the restaurant last night?"

"Yeah. For some reason the police didn't take him into custody. So I'd like to go pay him a visit this morning, ask him some questions."

"About what?"

"I don't think it's a coincidence that he worked for me, then disappeared right after your dad drowned."

Megan's eyes grew wide. "You think he had something to do with my dad's death?"

"I don't know. But he obviously had access to the boats here. Wade said he saw Kent working on Wednesday, but he never showed up on Thursday…or since."

"And you did seem suspicious of him last night."

"Yeah, I feel certain he's the one who tipped off the kitchen about us and the envelope."

"Which sort of turned out to be a good thing."

"Yeah, except that Kent is still out there."

* * *

After breakfast, while Garret went out to check on the marina and speak to his employees, Megan used the landline phone to call Arthur, the press operator at her father's newspaper. "Sorry to bother you on a Sunday and so early, but I—"

"You are not a bother, Megan. I don't ever want you to think such a thing."

"Well, I know you were Dad's right-hand man, Arthur. I know I can depend on you. And I didn't really tell you what I was looking for yesterday. I know I probably should've." She hadn't told Arthur, not because she didn't trust him, but because she didn't want to put him in danger.

"I think I know what you were looking for, Megan." He made a loud sigh. "Did your dad tell you much about his research? I mean into them Marco boys and the casino and whatnot?"

"Yes," she said eagerly. "I know all about that."

"And you're looking for the envelope?"

"Yes! Do you have any idea where it might be?"

"You don't have it?"

She explained all that they'd been through, all the way up to the faux envelope last night.

"I had no idea about all that, Megan—that you'd been in any sort of danger. Rory wouldn't like that. Not at all. How're you holding up?"

She told him about Garret's help.

"Garret Larsson is a good man," Arthur said. "Your dad trusted him."

"So do I."

She explained her plan about returning to the newspaper office to clean up and look around some more. "And I don't expect you to come," she said quickly. "I can ask someone from the police force to join me. I wouldn't expect you to miss church and—"

"Don't you worry about that, Megan. The good book says that when your ox falls in a ditch you can pull him out. Even on the Sabbath." He chuckled. "Besides, I don't go to church every Sunday. I'll call Barb, too. She goes to early church. I'm sure she'll want to help."

"Thanks, Arthur. I really appreciate it. And I'll still call for police protection."

"Barb knew Rory's habits better than anyone. She might have some ideas about his secret hiding places."

After she hung up, she and Garret went outside to talk to the policemen who'd been parked at the marina all night. Officer Harter assured them that he'd observed nothing. "And I have something for you," he told Megan as he produced her oversize bag still containing the faux envelope. They were both still damp. "Detective Greene thinks you should hold on to it."

She looked dubiously at the familiar bag, unsure she really wanted to keep toting that fake envelope around. Except that the bait had worked last night.

"Thanks." She took the bag, nervously swinging it back and forth.

"And he said to give you this, too." He held out an inexpensive flip phone and a charging cord. "He doesn't want you to be out of touch."

"Thank you!" She clutched the phone to her chest. "I wanted to get a new one, but the only cell phone store in town was closed."

"The number is taped inside, and Detective Greene's number as well as the police department's are already programmed."

She thanked him again.

"So what are your plans now?" he asked.

"First of all, we want to go to the hospital to check in on Lieutenant Conrad," Garret told him.

"I hear he's making a good recovery," the officer told them.

Megan explained her plan for the newspaper office. "A couple of newspaper employees agreed to meet me there at ten."

"And I hope to look up an ex-employee and have a talk with him." Garret gave the officer a slip of paper with Kent's address on it. "I'm not sure why the police didn't question him last night, but I think he's got something to hide."

The policeman's brows lifted. "You need backup?" he asked. "Our shift ends at eight o'clock, but I can get someone—"

"That'd be good."

"I hope we're not getting a false sense of security," Megan said as they got into his SUV.

"I know what you mean. We need to keep our guard up. I'm glad you'll have Arthur and Barb with you at the paper—as well as police protection."

"Yeah, that's reassuring. And my car should be at the paper, too. The tire store is closed today, but they had promised to park it back there when they were done."

"What about your keys? Got a spare set?"

"I asked them to drop my keys in the mail slot on the front door, and Arthur said he found them last night."

"Hopefully, your new tires are still intact," Garret said grimly.

"Yeah, I hadn't considered that." She grimaced at the thought of explaining more slashed tires to her insurance company. She examined the cell phone, relieved to see it was fully charged, then as Garret drove, she programmed a few numbers including Garret's, which she added to favorites for speed dialing. Feeling more secure, she tucked the phone into her zipped parka pocket, along with the other things she normally carried in her bag. Just to be safe.

The hospital, though a picturesque location overlooking the river, was a bit out of the way, but it was nearly visiting hours by the time they arrived.

"At least the cops are here." Garret pointed to the patrol car parked near the entrance. "Not sure if that's for us or someone visiting Michael. But reassuring."

Megan was tempted to leave her bait bag in the car, but knew that would be defeating its intended purpose, so instead she looped the strap over her shoulder and strolled toward the hospital.

"This fog is getting heavier," she said absently as Garret led the way between some parked cars. "Kind of puts a damper on the—" Her breath and words were wiped out as someone slammed her from behind. She let out a terrified scream as she smashed into a parked car, then tumbled down to the pavement.

EIGHTEEN

By the time Garret helped Megan to her feet, her bag and her attacker were gone. Along with the fake envelope. Garret ushered her over to the patrol car, relaying the information to the officers and pointing out the direction the attacker had gone. "I would've chased him," he said breathlessly, "but I was worried about Megan—didn't want to leave her alone."

The patrol car took off, and Garret turned his attention back to getting Megan safely inside the hospital. Once inside, he turned to stare intently into her eyes. "Are you sure you're okay? That was quite a fall you took."

She rubbed a sore elbow then tested the knee that had absorbed her tumble. "I think so."

"Want to get checked?" He pointed toward the ER with a half smile. "Lots of docs here."

"No, thank you." She frowned. "But now that they got our bait they'll know we were trying to trick them."

He nodded somberly. "I hope this doesn't make them believe we don't have the real papers. That was our safety net."

"I know."

"I'll get Michael's room number." He nodded as they walked into the hospital and toward the information desk.

"I want to get that for Michael." She pointed to a stuffed Curious George doll outfitted like a doctor that was in the gift shop window.

Garret grinned. "Great idea."

She went into the gift shop and took the plush toy to the register, picking out a get well card too. As she waited for the cashier, she noticed some interesting quilted bags hanging nearby. They had an ethnic look to them and were actually rather attractive.

"Those are made by a local woman who donates all the proceeds to Samaritan's Purse," the cashier informed her.

"What a fabulous idea." Megan fingered the sturdy fabric. "I support Samaritan's Purse, too." Suddenly, she remembered that her oversize bag had just been stolen and that her parka pockets were bulging with items in need of a handbag. She selected her favorite one and laid it on the counter just as Garret came into the shop. "I don't need a sack," she told the cashier, asking for scissors to remove the price tags.

"Nice," Garret said as he joined her.

"Handy, too." She gave him the monkey and card as she unloaded her pockets, putting the wallet and few other things into the bag. As they rode the elevator up, she noticed her disheveled image in the mirror, taking a moment to smooth her hair and even wipe some dirty smudges from one side of her face. "You didn't tell me I was a mess," she said teasingly to Garret.

"You look beautiful to me," he replied as the door slid open.

Her sore elbow and knee instantly felt better. And as they exited the elevator, she tried to imagine what their relationship might be like under normal circumstances. She hoped his kindness wasn't simply part of his chivalry and helpfulness.

"How about we don't mention that last assault to Michael," she suggested, pausing at the nurses' station to write in his card. "No need to worry him."

"I couldn't agree more."

To Megan's relief, Michael looked much better than the last time she'd seen him. They visited with him for a while, telling him recent details of the unsolved case, but trying to paint a more positive picture than Megan felt was real. Still, it was good to see him smiling. And it was good to hear his prognosis for a full recovery. But he soon grew tired and they told him goodbye.

"He seemed in good spirits," Megan said as they exited the hospital.

"But I can tell he's still working on the case." Garret cautiously looked left and right. "I could see the wheels spinning in his head while we told him about last night at Marco's."

"Maybe he'll come up with something helpful." She glanced around too.

"Stay near me." Garret wrapped an arm around her shoulders, holding her close. "And let's walk fast."

Soon they were inside his SUV, but Megan continued to keep a watchful eye while Garret drove them to town. Fortunately, they didn't see anyone following them and when they got to the newspaper, she was relieved to see that her car was parked in front and the tires were intact. She pointed to the patrol car parked conspicuously in front of her car. "And I've even got protection," she said as she got out.

"Even so, I'm going in with you," he insisted as he got out of the car, walking her to the door. But before she could insert her key, the door swung open and Arthur and Barb both welcomed her with warm hugs, and an armed officer sat in a nearby chair with a mug of coffee. "I can see you're in good hands," he said after he greeted the employees. "Call me if you need anything."

She promised to do so and then he exited the building with a feeling of determination brewing within him. He wanted to surprise Kent with this unexpected morning visit. Hopefully, getting caught off guard would help him to slip up. Garret's plan was to play oblivious. At least to start with. Then, if Kent wasn't cooperative, Garret would play tough.

He parked in front of the shabby-looking apartment complex and quickly surveyed the scene. To his relief, Kent's unit, although upstairs, was visible from the street. But as he went up the exterior stairs, Garret silently prayed. And then, without wasting a moment, he knocked firmly on the door.

When it opened, the stench of old cigarette smoke and filth rolled out and Kent, wearing a sleeveless T-shirt and boxers, looked red-eyed and reeked of alcohol. "Hey, Kent," Garret said cheerfully. "I was hoping we could talk."

"What about?"

"Well, for starters I've been concerned about you. Thought maybe you were sick or something."

"I'm not sick." Kent rubbed his unshaven chin. "What'd'ya want, anyway?"

"I'm just checking on my employee," Garret said evenly. "Want to know why you're not showing up for work. Or did you quit and forgot to tell me?"

Kent looked slightly confused.

"I mean, I noticed you're working at Marco's on the Waterfront now." Garret gave him a blank look.

"Yeah, but that's just nights."

"So you want to keep working for me?" Garret frowned doubtfully.

"I dunno." Kent glanced over his shoulder with a slightly nervous expression.

"Because I have to say, I'm not that impressed with your mechanical ability."

"Yeah, well…"

"What's going on with you and the Marco brothers?" Garret demanded. "Do you know about their mob connections or are you just one of their expendable pawns?" He leaned toward him with narrowed eyes.

"I don't have to talk to you." Kent started to close his door, but Garret blocked it with his foot.

"I'll take that as a yes," Garret said. "You're in deep with the Marco boys, aren't you? And that makes you a prime suspect in the murder of Rory McCallister."

The door opened a bit more. "You can't pin that on me."

Garret peered into his eyes. "I think I can. Wade just told me this morning that he remembers seeing you lurking around the marina on Thursday morning. And yet you didn't report for work that day. But you had access to Rory's boat. You had time to do something to it. I think that's what happened."

"You can't prove that."

"You're wrong, Kent," Garret bluffed. "The evidence is already stacking up against you. Your best hope is to come clean and see if the cops will cut you a break for—"

"Get outta here!" Kent yelled.

"I just wanted to give you a chance," Garret said calmly. "But looks like you'd rather do this the hard way."

Kent swore loudly and somewhat incoherently as Garret removed his foot from the doorway. The flimsy door slammed closed and Garret knew Kent was involved. He felt relieved to see other neighbors looking out, curious about the noise as he hurried away from the apartment complex. Once in his SUV, he called Detective Greene and shared this new information. "I think you should bring him in for questioning," Garret told him. "Scare him enough and you might get him to talk. Because I'm certain he was involved in Rory McCallister's so-called accident."

As Garret drove through town, he felt worried

about Megan and suddenly realized he hadn't bothered to get her new cell phone number. Although he knew she should be safe with Arthur and Barb with her at the newspaper office, he just wasn't certain. But when he called the newspaper's phone, Barb answered, assuring him that Megan was just fine.

"And the policeman's still there?"

"Working on another cup of coffee as we speak."

"How's the search going?" Garret asked. "Getting warmer?"

"No," she said glumly. "I really don't think that envelope is here."

"Yeah, that seems like the most obvious place, doesn't it? Rory was smarter than that."

"Do you want to talk to Megan?"

"Not right now. Just tell her I'm going back to the marina to take care of some business. But tell her to call me when she has a moment. I need to get her new cell phone number."

"Arthur and I are both so glad she has you to lean on, Garret. I know Rory would be very appreciative, too."

Garret thanked her and hung up. As he drove to the marina, keeping a lookout for anything suspicious, he thought about Rory. Had he even realized what a hornets' nest he'd poked into when he started his investigation? Had he ever considered that his life could be endangered, or his daughter's? Garret didn't think so. But he knew Rory well enough to know that he'd been impetuous and strong-willed. He marched into places that others avoided. Like David and Goliath, Rory had been unafraid to take on the giants in his life. Hopefully, his old friend's efforts wouldn't be for nothing.

It was close to one by the time Megan called. Her voice was tired and discouraged. "I'm done here and I just told Arthur and Barb to go home."

"So you'll be there alone?" Garret didn't like the sound of that.

"My armed guard is still here. Besides, I'm getting ready to leave, too."

"Why don't you meet me for lunch?" he said eagerly.

"That actually sounds good."

"How about The Bridgeview?" he suggested, remembering how he loved going there as a kid. "We could do it in memory of your dad."

"Oh, Garret, that sounds wonderful. Let's meet there."

"Only if you ask your armed guard to escort you."

"He looks like he might be ready for lunch, too." She chuckled.

"Whoever gets there first can save a table," Garret told her.

* * *

Despite her disappointment at not finding the envelope, Megan's spirits lifted as she thought about dining at The Bridgeview. What a great idea to eat there in honor of her dad. It was just what she needed. She hadn't seen the place in years. Hopefully, it wouldn't be too crowded because, even though the cool, foggy weather wasn't too welcoming, the tourists were still all over town.

With her police escort tailing her, she drove past Marco's on the Waterfront and shuddered. She had no desire to return there—ever. Not that they would care since they already had a line outside their entrance.

Driving on, she saw that The Bridgeview's parking lot held very few cars. Hopefully, they were open. She got out and hurried through the damp air, the haunting sound of the foghorn reminding her of her childhood. To her delight, the front door was open. But as soon as she stepped inside, she felt the difference. Something had changed in here.

Looking around, she could see the restaurant was run-down. The wood floors needed refinishing, the tables and chairs were worn and shabby and the walls looked dreary and sad. Even the restaurant's old owner, Marty, looked like he'd seen better days. Although his eyes lit up to see her.

"I'm surprised you're not busier," she said after they exchanged greetings. "Especially on Memorial Day weekend."

Marty just shook his head. "Between Marco's and the casino's restaurants, we haven't been too busy the past couple of years."

"I'm sorry."

"Yeah, I told the wife that if business doesn't pick up, we'll have to shut down."

"I sure hope that doesn't happen."

Megan spotted Garret entering the restaurant. "There's my, uh, lunch companion."

"Garret Larsson?" Marty nodded with approval. "Good for you, Megan. Good for both of you."

Megan's cheeks warmed at the insinuation. And yet she liked it, too. Who cared if someone assumed they were a couple? She smiled as she eagerly waved to Garret. Glad to be reunited with him, she felt safer as he came closer. Marty and Garret shook hands and before long they were ordering lunch—both of them chose fish and chips with coleslaw.

After Marty returned to the kitchen, Garret told her about Kent. "He had guilty written all over him." He scowled. "I can't believe I ever let Wade talk me into hiring him."

"Did Wade know what he was really like, what kind of person he was getting you involved with?"

Garret shook his head. "No, I don't think so. Wade isn't the sharpest crayon in the box, but he's not malicious. He doesn't like the Marco brothers any more than I do."

"Why didn't the police take Kent in last night?" Megan asked.

"Good question. Apparently they felt certain they had the two main suspects. Kent didn't interest them."

"So Kent is still out there…" Megan nervously twisted the paper napkin. "As well as the creep who knocked me down in the hospital parking lot…along with who knows how many other thugs." She glanced anxiously around the restaurant, where only a few tables were occupied, and then out over the river, where a thick blanket of fog was rolling in. She no longer felt safe. Not even with Garret there.

It wasn't long before Marty brought out their lunches. They thanked him and then Garret bowed his head and not only said a blessing, but also gave thanks for the life of Rory McCallister and asked God to help them bring justice to Cape Perpetua.

"Thank you for that prayer," Megan said quietly after they'd both said amen.

"Bon appétit," Garret said as he picked up a piece of fish.

Megan did likewise, giving it a contented sniff before taking a bite. "Yum," she said as she set the piece down. "Just as good as I remember."

For a while neither of them spoke much as they enjoyed their meal. Once again, Megan wished that they were involved in a real relationship, out for an afternoon date with nothing much to talk about beyond the weather and getting to know each other better. It sounded so blissful. Instead, they had this gloomy cloud hovering over them, sort of like the fog that now completely obliterated the river.

"The Bridgeview really does have the best fish and chips in town," he said as he shook out some malt vinegar.

"I agree." She picked up another piece of fish. "Dad said it's because Marty uses halibut. A lot of places use cod but it's not nearly as good."

"Your dad would agree." He chuckled. "I remember how he'd throw it back if he thought it would live. Otherwise he'd give it away."

Megan laughed—and then stopped. "Wait a minute!"

"Huh?" Garret stopped with a bite of coleslaw halfway between his mouth and the plate.

"I've got it." Her face flushed with excitement.

"Got what?"

She blotted her mouth with her napkin and stood "I know where the yellow envelope is, Garret. I'm certain of it."

"What? Where?"

She pushed her plate toward him. "Can you give Marty my apologies and ask him to put this in a to-go box?"

"But what are you—"

"I've got to go get it. Now!"

He reached out to grasp her arm. "Where is it?"

She leaned down, speaking quietly. "Dad hated cod. But when I reloaded his freezer yesterday, there was a large package marked cod."

He frowned. "So?"

"So, don't you remember how I told you Dad had once hid his novel manuscript in the freezer for safekeeping?"

"Oh, yeah." Garret nodded with wide eyes.

"I'm going out there now," she said.

"Not without me, you're not." He nodded over to the police escort who was still eating his lunch. "And not without him, either. I'll go let him know what's up."

Megan waited impatiently as Garret spoke to the cop. Jingling her car keys in front of Garret when he got back, she urged him to hurry.

"I'll just pay the bill, then follow you."

"Great. I just know this is it, Garret."

Megan's heart pounded with happy excitement as the three of them got into their vehicles and drove down Rawlins Road. She just knew this had to be it. It felt exactly like something her dad would do. If only the package was still there! In her eagerness, she knew she was driving too fast—but wasn't this an emergency? Nearly to the beach road turnoff, she realized that Garret had slowed down behind her. What was taking him so long? Didn't he know this was urgent? She turned onto the beach road, then slowed down so much that she was barely moving. But she still didn't see him turn yet, nor the policeman behind him. What was wrong?

NINETEEN

On Rawlins Road, Garret noticed the flashing lights behind him. As he pulled over for the oncoming cop car, he was well aware that Megan had been driving over the speed limit and that he'd been trying to keep up. But he should be able to explain to the cop what was going on. But the police car as well as an ambulance zipped past him. Now he felt a rush of panic. Had something happened to Megan?

No, that was impossible. She was less than a mile ahead of him. Probably wondering where he was. Seeing that the police car and emergency vehicles turned the opposite way on the beach road, he decided that they were off to help someone else and, once again, he stepped on it. He did not like having her out of his sight.

As he came to the intersection of the beach road, he looked in his rearview mirror again. Where was the cop who'd followed them from the restaurant? Shouldn't he be right behind him?

There was no point waiting for him. Leaving Megan on her own for even one minute seemed too long.

When Garret got to Rory's house, he was relieved to see Megan's Prius parked out in front—with her still in it. "What took you so long?" she demanded eagerly as he got out to meet her.

He explained about pulling over. "Maybe there's a wreck on the North Beach Road. Probably tourists."

Megan had her house key ready. "Let's hurry and get it and get out of here," she said, leading the way to the front door. "I just know it's in the freezer."

Garret looked up and down the quiet road. "I wish that cop would hurry," he said as he followed her to the house. "Maybe we should give Greene a call."

"Let's get the envelope first." Megan unlocked the door, letting them into the silent house. "Everything looks pretty much like it did yesterday," she said quietly.

Garret stepped in front of her in a protective way, reaching for his holster, making sure his firearm was ready—and wishing they'd waited for police backup.

As they quietly moved through the house, Megan could hear her heart beating in her ears. But fortunately, that was all she heard. Wasting no time, she headed straight for the garage and opened the freezer chest, desperately digging for the suspicious package of cod while Garret watched out the windows in the garage door, with his revolver ready. When she finally found the package, she tried to bend it in her hands and when it gave slightly, she knew it wasn't a frozen fish. It was paper. "This is it," she told Garret.

"Trouble," he said quietly, waving her over to him.

"What?" she asked nervously.

"That black sedan has both our cars blocked in."

As she peered out the garage door window, Megan shoved the package into her oversize bag. "There are two guys. They're going in the front door," she whispered in horror. "I left it unlocked."

"And these guys are armed," Garret whispered back. "We have to get out of here."

Megan dug in her roomy bag, producing her dad's Jeep key. "We can take the Jeep."

Garret pointed a ways down the beach road. "Look at that."

She peered down at a similar sedan parked down the road. Like it was waiting for them.

"What do we do?" she asked him.

"Take the old river road."

"Do you think we can make it? No one uses that road. It's a mess."

"That's one reason those sedans won't be able to follow us."

She nodded, waiting as he quietly opened the side door of the garage. "You're going to drive," he told her.

"Why?"

He held up his gun in answer. "I'll be riding shotgun."

Garret slipped out first, looking all around before motioning for her to join him. Together they went along the side of the garage until they reached the front, where Garret peered around the corner.

"We'll have to make a run for the Jeep. The driver's side is away from them. You stay low and get over there and unlock it while I back you up from here. As soon as you're inside, start the engine and I'll sprint over and jump in." Fortunately, the Jeep was only about ten feet from the garage. Still, it felt like fifty yards as she raced for the driver's door. Thanks to her trembling hands, it took longer than it should've to get inside and start the engine. But Garret seemed to literally fly over, jumping inside just as she put it in Reverse, backing right onto the lawn. Then, spinning it around, she tore off down the driveway and toward the old river road.

"The sedan on the road has seen us," Garret told her. "They're coming fast. Step on it."

Without speaking, she ran the Jeep through the gears and sped to the end of the beach road. Most people assumed the road ended there. The driver of the sedan was probably no different.

She had to slow down to turn off the beach road, but as the tires hit the sand and rocks, she put it into four-wheel drive and, thankful that Dad had been her driving instructor, she stepped on it again.

"You're doing great, Megan. Go!"

She pushed the Jeep as fast as it could safely go, praying that they wouldn't bounce off the bumpy road and wind up in the river where it looked like the tide was heading out.

When they finally had what seemed a cautious distance behind them, Megan slowed down a bit and glanced into the rearview mirror.

"They're not following," Garret said. "But we're not out of harm's way. All a person needs to do is check a GPS to see where this road ends."

"Where's that?" She held tightly to the steering wheel, trying to keep the Jeep on the bumpy road.

"Less than a mile from the marina. It won't take a genius to figure out where we're going." Garret was on the phone now, talking to Detective Greene, telling him they had the evidence and where they were headed. "If you could meet us there, we would appreciate it."

Megan continued pushing the Jeep, eager to get to the marina where the police would meet them. Although she felt a sense of accomplishment for how they'd gotten into her dad's house and nabbed that envelope, she didn't want them to play the heroes in this scenario. She would be happy to hand off the evidence to the police.

"I still can't believe we got it," she said.

"Want me to make sure it's the real deal?" Garret offered.

"Yes, please, do."

In no time he confirmed it was Rory's research packet.

"I will only turn it over to the police if they promise to let me have a copy. I need to finish what my dad started." And then she would get on with her life. Whatever that meant. She wasn't completely sure. Something about being back in her beloved little seaside town...and something about Garret...made her question returning to Seattle. But there was no time to examine those doubts now.

By the time they reached the end of the old river road, Megan felt like her brain had been seriously rattled by all the bumps.

"I thought the cops were meeting us here," she said.

"I did, too. But maybe they're at the marina."

So she hightailed it to the marina, hoping that Detective Greene and other cops would be waiting for them. But when she spied the marina from the road, the parking lot by the store looked barren.

"Huh?" Garret looked all around. "Where are they?"

"I don't know." She glanced at him. "What should I do?"

"We'll go in and wait for them." Garret shook his head. "At least there are no black sedans waiting for us."

"Yeah. That's something."

"You must've driven even faster than they expected," Garret said as she turned in at the marina. "Nice work. Park in front of the store for now. I've been worried about Wade. I want him with us. Then we'll park the Jeep by the house and hole up there."

Megan felt relieved as she parked right next to the store. "We made it."

"You did great," Garret told her. "Give Greene a call. Tell him we'll be in the house. I'll be back in less than a minute." He jumped out and ran to the store.

Garret had just stepped into the store when

Megan felt icy fingers tightening around her throat. She turned to see a familiar-looking man outside the Jeep. He'd stuck his hand through the cut part of the Jeep's soft top.

"Come on out, Miss McCallister," he said in a sinister tone, waving a revolver with his other hand. "And bring your bag with you."

Before she could respond, he whipped open the door, jerked her out and grabbed the bag with the envelope. Then, twisting her left arm painfully, he shoved the barrel of his gun into her ribs, thrust her bag into her free hand and commanded her to walk down the dock.

"You're the guy at Marco's restaurant," she said suddenly. "You're Kent Jones. Garret's employee."

Ignoring her, he just kept forcing her down the dock. She desperately tried to think of something—some way to catch him off guard and escape.

"Garret told me that you had access to my dad's boat," she said as he pushed her along.

"I had access to all the boats." He stopped by a midsize fishing dory.

With one big shove, he pushed her into the boat. Megan landed on her back next to some gas cans, but quickly struggled to her feet only to discover he was on deck, too. With his revolver still pointed at her.

"Down on the deck. Now! And keep your mouth shut or I'll be forced to use this." He waved his gun. Then he shoved her back down into a mess of coiled ropes. With one hand he hurried to pull in his line then started the motor. He grabbed her by the arm and forced her up to the bow, shoving her into a seat. "I want you next to me." He gave her an evil grin. "Just like we're on a hot date." He chuckled creepily, then narrowed his eyes as he flashed his gun again. "But don't move. And don't get any ideas."

She was still clutching the bag with the precious envelope as the boat took off down the river—still trying to think of a way out of this mess. But first she wanted information. "You did something to my dad's boat, didn't you?"

He feigned an innocent look as he steered the boat out into the thick fog.

"You did, didn't you?" she persisted, clutching her bag to her chest. "You made it sink. I know you did."

"Not me personally," he said lightly. "But my gun helped out." He snickered and waved his gun.

"So you killed my dad?" She tried to keep her voice calm as if she was doing an interview for the paper.

"Nah. That was someone else."

"Did they drug him?" she asked in a flat tone. "Poison?"

"Something like that. Let's just say ol' Rory barely knew what hit him."

As Kent focused on getting the boat down the river, she began to formulate a plan. A plan which might or might not work. Despite the thick fog, she could see that the current was moving at a good clip—because the tide was still going out. The good news was that the water level would be low. If she could jump out on the starboard side, she might be able to swim underwater long enough to make it to the shallows where Kent wouldn't be able to maneuver his boat. Although since it was a dory, he might be able to go farther than she expected. But hopefully, the fog would help cover her while she swam for shore. Still, there was no time to waste. He was already beyond the marina.

Clutching the bag to her chest, she slid out the envelope and slipped it into her parka as the gunman's attention was fixed solidly on the fog-encased river. Then she called upon her acting skills. She made a gagging sound. "I'm gonna be sick!" she exclaimed.

"What?" He turned to look at her and she gave her best imitation of nausea.

"I'm seasick! I'm gonna throw up." She threw her bag down on the deck, knowing she was leaving her phone and wallet behind, but knowing she couldn't take it. Then cupping her hand over her mouth, she feigned an even louder gagging noise that sounded so real, she wasn't sure she was faking. In fact, she honestly felt sick.

Still gripping the helm, Kent scowled at her then tipped his head to the railing. "Don't barf on my boat or I'll make you clean it up."

She dashed over to the starboard side and, hanging her head over the railing, she made some loud and realistic noises while tightening the waist belt of her parka to secure the envelope and then, just as he turned the boat toward the middle of the river, she tumbled over the side. The shock of the cold water nearly sucked her breath away, but instead of surfacing like she wanted to do, she swam with all her might until she felt certain her lungs were going to burst.

She gasped for air when her head finally emerged from the water, hoping that she'd gone far enough to escape him. But she could still see the dark outline of his boat and she could hear his engine rumbling not that far away. When a couple of gunshots splashed the water just a few feet from her, she took a fast gulp of air then ducked back under, praying for strength and help.

But as she swam for what she hoped was the river's edge, she felt nothing but the current moving her. And it was going even faster than she'd expected. If Kent didn't shoot her the next time she popped up, she would probably be pulled out into the ocean. Not that she would last that long with these water temps. Begging God for help, she swam as hard as she could, but she knew that when she surfaced, Kent would probably be even closer, his gun ready to stop her.

TWENTY

Garret felt a rush of alarm to see Megan was no longer in Rory's Jeep. Where had she gone? He'd been in the store less than a minute, calling for Wade, who appeared to be missing, as well. Had they both gone to the house together? He was about to go see when he heard someone yelling.

"Hey!" a male voice called out. "Over here!"

Garret peered through the fog, trying to see the man waving at him from the dock.

"Somebody's hurt!" the man yelled.

Thinking it was Megan, Garret ran down toward him. "Who is it?" he demanded. "What happened?" As he got closer, he saw the caller was Mike Fowler, an older guy who docked his boat here.

"I don't know," Mike said, leading Garret to the end of the dock. "I was working on my boat when I heard someone moaning and groaning. He's right there." Mike pointed down at a small fishing boat.

Garret looked down to see Wade rubbing his head with a bewildered expression. "What happened to you?" He climbed in to help Wade to his feet.

"Kent showed up." Wade wobbled a little as he stood. "Had a gun. He made me come down here then he whacked me on the head. That's the last I remember."

Garret turned back to Mike. "Did you see anything?"

Mike shrugged. "I sure didn't see that."

"But did you see anyone on the dock?"

Mike rubbed his chin. "Yeah, there was a man and woman just a little bit ago."

"Did the woman have reddish hair?" Garret demanded.

"Yep. She sure did. Pretty, too." He described the man, and Garret knew it was Kent.

"Where did they go?"

"I went below before they got down this far. But I did hear a boat take off. Thought that was odd since we're so fogged in. Who'd wanna go fishing on the river now? And with the red-flag warning, no one in his right mind would head for the ocean but it did sound like they went downriver." He grimly shook his head.

"Give me a hand with him," Garret commanded Mike, and together they got Wade onto the dock. "Take him to the store and call 911.

Explain what happened and that I went after the boat. Tell them to send out the coast guard."

Mike nodded as he supported Wade. "So this is serious?"

"Oh, yeah!" Garret turned away, running for his boat. He jumped in and within two minutes he was pulling away from the dock and heading downriver. Mike was right. This was no day for fishing or going on the ocean. But there were a number of coves and home docks between here and the sea. It was possible Kent had taken Megan to one of those spots to lie low.

Garret prayed as he navigated down the river. Barely able to see in what his grandma would have called pea soup, he couldn't go fast. He knew the odds of finding Megan were minuscule, and so as he trolled along, he prayed. After he prayed, he had to ask himself questions. Why would Kent kidnap Megan? She must've had Rory's envelope on her. Why not just steal that and let Megan go? Except that she would've seen him and could identify him. And in that case, what would Kent do with her? Garret hated to think about that. Better to focus on finding her. That meant finding Kent's boat.

The low tide was starting to ebb now, making the water fairly smooth and calm. Garret turned off his motor to just listen, hoping to pick up the sound of Kent's motor and head in that direction. But he heard nothing but the water slapping against the side of the boat as the current carried him along. Was it possible that Kent had taken his dory over the bar? The ocean wasn't really that rough today, but visibility was terrible. Of course, Kent could land his dory on any sandy stretch of beach. And thanks to the weather, Garret's chances of finding him were about zero.

As his boat continued drifting downriver, Garret thought he could maybe hear the low rumble of a boat motor. He strained his ears to listen. Was it possible that Kent was nearby? And where was the coast guard?

Garret looked downriver, trying to see the form of a small boat. He knew that Kent, like him, wouldn't be using his running lights. Garret patted his revolver, thankful he'd strapped it on before going to lunch. He considered starting his motor again, but knew that noise would draw unwanted attention. If Kent was up ahead, it would be better to slowly sneak up on him. But what then? A shootout would endanger Megan.

Garret noticed a floating log up ahead. Not so unusual this time of year, but not something a boater wanted to encounter. It could wreak havoc on propellers. Not that he was concerned since his motor wasn't running, but he didn't want to risk the sound of the floating log clunking against his metal hull. So he reached for a paddle and, leaning over the starboard side of the bow, he was prepared to push it away with the paddle.

But as he got closer, he realized this was not just a log. There was something blue on it. And as he got even closer, he realized it was a woman. "Megan!" he said in a hushed voice. Her head popped up and their eyes locked. "Be quiet," he warned as he went to grab a line. "Catch this," he instructed as he prepared to throw it to her.

It took several tries, but she eventually got it and he quickly pulled her toward his boat, thanking God with each tug. "Try to be quiet," he said as he reached for her hands to hoist her onto his boat.

"Thank God," she mumbled as they embraced. She was white as a sheet and shivering with cold as he helped her to a seat. He removed his own coat, wrapping it around her. And then he went to a stowage bench where he dug out an emergency blanket, wrapping that over her, as well. "Get low," he whispered. "I can hear a motor running nearby. I'm guessing it's Kent."

She nodded and, following his instructions, got down on the deck. Huddling with the coat and blanket still around her, she looked like a small, frightened child, and everything in him wanted to get down beside her to comfort her.

But he knew if they were going to make it out of this, he needed to move—and move fast.

"I'm going to have to run my engine now," he quietly explained as he got ready to start it. "It'll make some noise so I'm going to gun it and really take off. But I know that Kent's dory has a big engine. I'm guessing he'll follow."

She nodded with wide eyes. "He's got a gun."

"Yeah, I heard." He leaned down to look into her eyes. "Pray for us, Megan." And then he kissed her forehead and felt relieved to see her smile. Then he started his engine. To his relief it started without a hitch. He went for the helm and immediately turned the boat toward the marina. But with only his compass to guide him, he couldn't be positive.

He heard the other boat engine revving and he knew that Kent would be in hot pursuit, but he hadn't expected him to get here so quickly—or to be so close to the town side of the river. Garret knew that Kent was trying to cut him off by positioning himself between Garret and the marina.

He tried to think as he pushed his boat even faster. There was no way he was going to outrun Kent. And now he could see the dark outline of Kent's dory on the leeward side, quickly catching up. Garret felt like they were a sitting duck now and, just as he suspected, Kent began to shoot.

Garret saw water starting to pour through the bullet holes and knew he needed to think fast. Suddenly, he remembered a spit of land on the other side of the river that was exposed at low tide. It was possible that Kent wouldn't know about it. But with water coming in fast, there was little time to think.

Garret gunned his engine to full throttle and took off across the river, hoping and praying that he was close to the spit, but knowing it was a long shot. The boat was filling fast, slowing down—and Kent was in fast pursuit. Garret pulled out his gun now and let loose with several shots, praying he'd hit Kent's boat and it, too, would start filling with water. Naturally these shots were returned.

"We're gonna have to jump," Garret told Megan as he turned the boat upriver. "Think you can swim again?" She leaped to her feet, joining him in the bow as he used a line to secure the helm to keep the boat headed upriver.

"The boat goes one way and we go the other," he quickly explained as he took her hand, leading her to the side. "Ready?"

Together they went over the railing and into the fast-moving cold water. Meanwhile, Garret's boat continued upriver. As more shots were fired, it was clear that Kent was not giving up. And based upon the shots splashing into the nearby water, Garret felt certain Kent had spotted them. No way could they outswim the dory! And with little visibility and no sign of land nearby, Garret didn't know if they'd even jumped out in the right spot. Were they about to die together?

TWENTY-ONE

Megan had never been so cold or tired in her life, but the feeling of sandy loam river bottom beneath her feet gave her hope. Suddenly, they both were trudging out of the river, falling down onto the sandy shore, coughing and sputtering and gasping.

"Are you okay?" Garret reached for her hand.

"I guess," she said breathlessly as he pulled her to her feet. Did he really expect her to walk now? Her legs felt like overcooked spaghetti.

"We gotta get out of sight." He tugged her back into the water.

"No more," she protested in exhaustion. "Can't swim."

"Wading," he explained. "To hide our footprints."

"Oh." She clung to what little warmth was in his hand as he led her through the shallow water. She was so cold she could barely feel her feet and she'd long since lost her shoes. Finally, they came to a reedy area and Garret began to lead them inland, eventually collapsing amongst the taller reeds. Megan flopped backward and Garret flopped down beside her.

"We should be out of sight here," he said wearily.

"Where are we?" She was still trying to catch her breath.

"I'd hoped to find a spit," he explained. "Not even sure this is it. But maybe it doesn't matter."

"I'm so cold." Megan shivered.

Garret sat up, pulling her close to him as he wrapped his arms around her. "Let's keep each other warm if we can."

Megan didn't resist as she snuggled up against him and, whether it was from body heat or just the closeness of a man she had feelings for, she did begin to feel warmer. "Thank you for rescuing me," she said quietly. "I don't think I would've made it otherwise."

"I could hardly believe my eyes when I saw you on that log," he murmured. "God must've been watching out for us."

For a while they just sat there in the reeds, holding on to each other and trying to get warm. Although she was still shivering, Megan didn't think she was going to die from hypothermia. Well, depending on how long they had to remain here. She looked past the reeds to the foggy river.

She couldn't see the other side, but suspected that they were just a mile or so past town. That meant there should be a few houses nearby.

"So what are we going to do now?" She could feel her breathing growing more normal. "Should we hike out and look for help?" She looked at her soggy socks, wondering how far she could actually hike. To her surprise Garret still had on his athletic shoes, but he was shivering. She realized she had on his coat and started to remove it.

"No, you keep it on," he said.

She tried not to stare as he removed his long-sleeved knit shirt, wringing it out. She couldn't help but notice he was in good shape as he pulled it back on. "That'll help some." He pointed to one of the pockets on his coat. "My phone should be in there."

She unzipped and removed it, handing it to him.

He messed with it, but finally set it aside. "It's shot." Now he removed his Ruger from his holster, carefully checking it out.

"Is your gun toast, too?"

"It might still work." He emptied the two remaining bullets then blew through the chamber, looking down the barrel. Now he pulled out more bullets and, after rolling them between his hands and blowing on them, started to reload them into his gun.

"Do you really think you could shoot him?" she asked quietly.

"Kent?" Garret shrugged as he closed the chamber. "I wouldn't want to kill him. Or anyone, for that matter. But I don't mind stopping him from killing us."

"He admitted to being involved in my dad's death," she said grimly.

"You're kidding?" Garret's brows arched. "He actually confessed that?"

"Yeah. That's when I knew he planned to kill me. Otherwise he wouldn't have disclosed that. Don't you think?"

He barely nodded. "What did he say?"

"He admitted helping to sink Dad's boat. Said he did it with his gun. Someone else did something to Dad. Somehow knocked him out. Kent said he never even felt it." She shuddered. "I imagined a hypodermic needle."

"And based on what we heard about the autopsy, I'm guessing no one noticed." Garret shook his head.

"And no toxicology," she said sadly.

"Well, at least we have a general idea of what happened." Garret looked up and down the river. "I can't tell if this is the spit or not, but the tide is starting to come in. If it is the spit, it will eventually be under water."

"We should probably move," Megan said. "In case Kent comes back."

"Just what I was thinking." He stood, helping Megan to her feet.

"And if this isn't the spit—if it's land—we might be able to find a house and use a phone."

He pointed to her socks. "Can you walk in those?"

"My feet are so numb, I probably won't feel anything, anyway."

He visibly shivered and Megan unzipped his coat. "Here, take this. I'm already starting to warm up a little. I don't need two coats."

He reluctantly took it, adjusting his gun holster before he zipped it up. "Let's go."

He led her through the reeds and after a fairly short distance they came to water. "It must be the spit," she told him. "You were right."

"Well, that's amazing. But that means we'll be stuck here. Unless you want to swim."

She shuddered. "How far is it?"

"A lot farther than it was to get here."

"I honestly don't know if I can make it, Garret." She felt close to tears. "But if you think you can make it, maybe I could wait here."

"I'm not leaving you alone. Besides, the coast

guard should be here soon. And then I'll shoot an emergency shot."

"You mean if your gun works."

"It'll work," he said in a less than certain tone, peering out over the water. "But I really thought they'd be here by—" He grabbed her arm, pulling her down to the damp sand and holding a forefinger over his lips. "Hear that?" he said quietly.

She listened then nodded. "Maybe it's the coast guard," she said in a hushed tone.

But he simply shook his head. "Wrong motor."

"Kent?"

He nodded grimly, pointing upriver to where she could see the shadowy outline of a dory slowly rumbling toward them. Did Kent suspect they were on this spit? Had he spotted the place where they'd come out of the water? Was he circling the spit? She knew the spit wasn't very wide, but wondered how long it was, if there was any place to hide on it. Maybe back in the taller reeds, although she felt too afraid to move as the menacing shadow continued to approach.

"You said this was a spit," she whispered in his ear. "Doesn't that mean it's attached to land?"

"Only at minus tide," he whispered back. "Not today."

"Can we get back into the high reeds?" she asked.

"Not without being seen. Don't move." Garret silently unzipped his black parka, slowly spreading it like wings to shield her more visible blue parka from the boat.

Kneeling on the ground behind his open parka, Megan shivered and prayed. She prayed that the dory would just keep on going…and that the coast guard was on their way. But to her horror, the engine slowed down and the next thing she knew, Garret was pushing her to her feet. "To the reeds," he said as they took off, the sound of gunshots following them.

They dove into the reeds, but the gunshots continued. "Should we go to the other side of the spit?" she asked. "So he'd have to go around?"

"He's in a dory," Garret said as he removed his gun. "He can land it on the sand."

"Oh, yeah."

"And it sounds like that's what he's doing." Garret held up his gun, clearly getting ready to aim and to shoot.

"Do you think it'll really work?" she whispered fearfully.

"Pray that it does."

But before she could pray, she saw the silhouette of a man clomping through the reeds toward them. As he got closer, she knew it was Kent. And besides a handgun, he appeared to have a rifle, too. Garret raised his revolver and pulled the trigger. Nothing!

TWENTY-TWO

Garret spun the chamber and tried it again. To his relief a shot rang out and Kent dropped to the ground. Whether it was from a bullet wound or just an attempt to take cover, Garret couldn't be sure. But he didn't want to stick around and find out. "Let's run," he said to Megan. "Keep your head low and go fast. I'll cover you and be right behind you."

"Are you sure?"

"Yes. Go across and then turn to your right and go as far as the spit allows."

As she took off, Garret kept his eyes pinned on the spot where Kent had hit the ground. If he was unhurt, he would probably stand up and take some more shots. For a couple of seconds nothing happened, but then—to Garret's shocked surprise—Kent leaped to his feet and was less than ten yards away. Suddenly, he was running toward Garret with his rifle aimed directly at him.

* * *

Megan had just turned right, like Garret had instructed, when she heard the exchange of gunshots behind her. She stopped in her tracks as a rush of fresh terror ran through her, followed by questions. What if Garret's gun wasn't working properly? What if Kent had shot and wounded Garret? Should she return to help him? Or would that simply complicate things? Or what if Garret was dead? She couldn't bear to dwell on the last question. *Just keep going*, she told herself as she ran along the wet, sandy beach. She could see that this spit was steadily shrinking with the incoming tide. Eventually it would be covered in water. But by then…it probably wouldn't matter, anyway.

Determined to do as Garret had told her, she continued to run. She had no idea where she was going exactly, or what good it would do—besides temporarily evading Kent. But how long could that last? Finally, she saw the end of the spit. She slowed to a walk, catching her breath, and was suddenly shaken by more gunfire. Several shots that split the silence of the fog. What was going on back there? Was Garret okay?

At the end of the spit, she fell to her knees, gasping for air and praying for God to help Garret. "Please, God! Spare him!" she prayed between breaths, hot tears streaking down her cold cheeks. "Keep him safe! For me! Please!" Suddenly, she heard the sound of a boat engine. Peering through the fog, she recognized the silhouette. It was the same dark fishing boat that had shot at them at Garret's house, then later by the bridge, nearly killing Michael. Kent had probably called them for backup.

She knew she needed to look for cover, but her options were the reeds, which were too far away, or the fog, which seemed unlikely. She got down low, wishing her parka wasn't such a bright shade of blue—and wishing she'd thought to remove the package still tucked beneath it. If she was killed, the mob would have custody of the incriminating documents. Her father's story would die with her.

Garret's shots had managed to slow Kent down, giving Garret the chance to put some distance between them as he ran through the reeds. His plan was to reach the tallest reeds, get down low and reload his Ruger—and be ready for him this time. He'd wasted most of his rounds during their last skirmish, by aiming for Kent's legs, hoping to knock him down and incapacitate him. But Kent had returned fire, forcing Garret to shoot carelessly—using up his bullets. But at least it had waylaid Kent, giving him something to think about. And fortunately, Kent's aim wasn't any better than Garret's.

Breathing hard, Garret thought about Megan. She should've reached the end of the spit by now. But what next? The spit was already shrinking in the incoming tide. They certainly couldn't remain here for too long. But could they possibly survive the swim to land? With the cold, churning water of the incoming tide against the flowing river, he didn't think so.

He strained his ears and realized that the reeds nearby were moving. And not from the wind, since it was completely still. Once again, he got his revolver ready, holding it steady and pointing it in the direction of the rustling reeds. He'd kill Kent—but only to protect Megan. He would rather wound him. It would be more satisfying to see his ex-employee suffer trial and conviction and jail.

As soon as Garret spotted the dark image trudging through the reeds, he lifted his gun and, taking aim at the lower half of Kent's body, released two shots—rewarded by a scream of pain as Kent crumbled to the ground.

Determined not to waste a moment, or give Kent time to respond, Garret took off and, staying low, ran through the reeds toward the other side of the spit. But as he came to the steadily shrinking beach, he could hear the sound of a boat motor. It did not sound like the coast guard—and it sounded like it was on the other end of the spit—right where he had sent Megan.

Garret ran full speed, praying as he went, and knowing full well that his single revolver would be no match for the weapons he suspected were onboard the fishing boat. He was almost there when he heard another sound—more engines, bigger ones—and he realized the coast guard was approaching.

With his Ruger still in his hand, Garret stopped and fired three shots into the air as a distress signal, hoping to get the coast guard's attention. He continued moving toward the end of the spit, reloading his gun, then paused again, firing three more shots—praying that they would figure it out.

Out in the open now, Garret crouched low, making his way toward the end of the spit, praying that he'd find Megan and that she'd be okay. Suddenly, he saw a flash of blue through the fog and then, running directly to her, he fell to the ground beside her, making her jump. "It's just me," he said as used himself and his black coat to conceal and protect her. "Are you all right?" he asked quietly.

"Yes," she whispered back. "I am now. But that boat's out there—the one that shot at us—"

"The coast guard is out there, too," he reassured her.

"Kent?"

"I wounded him. Should slow him down some." Garret could feel her shivering, probably from both the cold and fear. Hopefully, he could help abate that. She was a sturdy woman, but he knew that anyone could go into shock. And so he began to pray aloud, quietly, but with faith.

As Megan shivered beneath the layers of heavy wool emergency blankets, she couldn't believe they were finally safe. Was it even possible? Everything had happened so quickly. One minute she thought it was the end—and suddenly it all changed when not just one, but three coast guard boats had shown up. Her memory of the details was even more foggy than the weather, but it hadn't taken long for the coast guard boats to surround the fishing boat and then take the three armed men from the boat into custody. Not a shot was fired.

The only thing she could clearly remember was the kiss. In the same moment they knew their ordeal was over, Garret had gathered her into his arms and holding her close, they had kissed so long and so passionately that she actually began to feel warm again.

They were still kissing when the coast guard

sent the surf boat ashore. Their rescuers laughed in amusement as they interrupted the kiss, assuring them they would have time to finish it later. Now, with the coast guard still searching for Kent on the spit, Megan and Garret were nearly back at the marina.

With one arm around Megan, Garret had been telling one of the officers what had happened. But now the boat had stopped and they were suddenly disembarking at the marina, where several cop cars were parked in front of the store. "I'll let you inside so you can get warm and dry," Garret said as he rushed her toward his house. Detective Greene waved to them, running to catch up, telling them to wait. "I have questions."

"Megan is nearly hypothermic," Garret said. "She can talk to you after she gets warmed up."

Greene looked at both of them. "Yeah, sure, you both should get into dry clothes." He walked along with them, going inside. "I'll just wait in here, if you don't mind."

With her teeth chattering uncontrollably, Megan just nodded, hurrying to the master suite, where she peeled of her soggy clothes. The package that she'd kept with her the whole time was a little worse for wear. But, worried it might still disappear, she took it into the bathroom with her and securely locked the door.

After a long hot shower, she emerged into

the steamy bathroom. Worried that her dad's precious research would be ruined from the water, she eagerly tore into it. To her relief, inside the soggy yellow envelope, the documents themselves were sealed in an oversize Ziploc bag. She smiled to remember her dad's cautious ways. Of course he'd thought to protect these papers.

Before long, she joined Detective Greene and Garret and together they told him the whole story. Megan held up the papers, still sealed in the plastic bag. "I'm willing to hand these over to you, but only if I can make copies first."

Detective Greene nodded. "Why don't we go to the station to make them? We'll be safe there."

"You think we're still in danger?" Megan asked.

"We've got a lot of guys in custody, but we haven't taken in the kingpins yet." He pointed to the bag. "Hopefully, that will give us what we need to do that."

"I'm sure it will," Garret told him.

By the time they returned to the marina, it was dark. "I think we should both sleep well tonight," Garret told Megan, pointing to the patrol car still parked in front of the marina. Greene had promised round-the-clock protection until the rest of Marco's mob was in custody—including the brothers.

"I'm so tired I think I could sleep through an earthquake."

Despite his reassurances, Garret looked all around as they made their way to the house. He suspected he'd be doing that for a while. He took a long look at the dock, noticing the empty slip where his little fishing boat was usually docked. According to the coast guard it was entirely fixable and would be returned to him for repairs on Tuesday. Fortunately, that wasn't his only boat.

Once inside they worked together to make a nice little dinner that they quietly ate at the breakfast bar.

"I can't believe it's over." She shook her head. "Or almost."

"Rory really got the goods on the Marco brothers. They weren't just skimming from the casino, although that seems to be considerable, they were trafficking drugs, as well. He had all kinds of proof—letters, photographs, statements, you name it. Valuable stuff. I had no idea he had gathered that much."

"Dad was always thorough."

"It was fun seeing Detective Greene so impressed."

She smiled. "That would've pleased Dad."

"Seeing all these guys being arrested would've made him pretty happy, too."

She looked into Garret's eyes. "Thanks so much. I never could've done it without you."

"We made a pretty good team." Garret longed to take this relationship further, but knew he needed to pace himself. She'd been through so much today. They both needed a good night's sleep. "It's the Memorial Day parade tomorrow," he said as he gathered up their dishes. "Do you want to go?"

"Of course." She smiled. "Wouldn't miss it." Now she frowned. "Well, if it's safe. Do you think the police will have taken in the others by then?"

"It sounded like they were rounding them up tonight."

She closed her eyes with a deep sigh. "I sure hope so."

Garret wanted to ask her about what would happen after tomorrow, after her dad's memorial service on Wednesday, after everything was all wrapped up for her in Cape Perpetua. Would she still put the newspaper and Rory's house up for sale like she had said originally? Maybe the last few days would make her glad to leave…glad to get back to a calmer, quieter life in Seattle. He wanted the answers to all his questions, but he knew she was weary. This was not the time.

* * *

Megan felt like her old self the next morning. And, after receiving news from Detective Greene—that six more men had been taken into custody, including Kent and the Marco brothers and two of their sons—she was eager to go to the Memorial Day parade. And it was fun watching it with Garret. The festivities reminded her of her childhood. Dad had always loved this parade, often participating with a float representing the newspaper.

In the afternoon Megan excused herself from Garret, explaining that she had work to do at the newspaper. "My car's there," she told him. "And Arthur offered to come in to keep me company." She slipped the new flip phone Detective Greene had loaned to her into the bag that had been retrieved from Kent's impounded boat. "I'll probably be there most of the day working on Dad's article." She smiled at him, realizing she didn't really want to be away from him for that long, but knowing there was work to be done.

"I've got work to catch up on here at the marina, too," Garret told her. "But if you finish the article in time, maybe you'd let me take you to dinner."

"At The Bridgeview?" she asked hopefully.

He nodded. "To make up for our interrupted lunch the other day."

"It's a date." She looked slightly embarrassed. "I mean, yeah, I'll meet you there. Want to say 6:30?"

"It's a date." He grinned.

As she drove to the newspaper office, she was already working on the first article in her head. She knew that it would take more than just one article to tell the story of what had gone on in Cape Perpetua these past couple of years. She planned to do exposés on the casino, the Marco mafia, the restaurant used for money laundering, as well as the drug-smuggling ring. With only two days before publication day, she knew she'd have to write fast. But she thought she could do it. And her final article would be a piece about her dad, her family and their commitment to bringing the news to Cape Perpetua for nearly a hundred years. A tradition that was coming to an end this week.

TWENTY-THREE

Megan was happily exhausted after two solid days of writing articles for the paper. Plus, she'd accomplished much more than expected in that short time, only leaving for dinner dates with Garret—the highlight of her day. She knew her writing progress had to be due to the lack of distractions—that and the comfort of sitting with her laptop in Dad's old office. But with only Arthur on Monday, and then Barb, as well, on Tuesday, she was able to keep her nose to the grindstone as Dad would say. And she felt certain he would be pleased with her. Maybe even proud. She hoped so.

"You done good," Arthur told her as he prepared to put the paper to bed on Tuesday evening. "You're your father's daughter."

She thanked him with a hug. Then she thanked Barb for her moral support and multiple cups of coffee as well as homemade lunches and snacks.

"You're the best," she said as she hugged her. "I wish I could take you to Seattle with me."

"So you're really leaving us?" Arthur frowned with dismay.

Megan pursed her lips. She really wasn't sure about this decision. Despite her promise to be back to work by next Monday, she was torn. Not only in regard to the newspaper. She was torn over her strong feelings for Garret, as well. The problem was that she just wasn't certain that he shared those same feelings. Oh, she knew he liked her well enough. He'd never made a secret of that. But despite the one kiss they'd shared, he hadn't made the slightest attempt toward romance over the last two days. And she had given him opportunity.

On one hand, she respected him for that. She'd never been a fan of those guys who came on too strong. Plus, she'd had a lot going on emotionally. But last night, after a late dinner at The Bridgeview, she had stood in front of him in the parking lot, longing to be kissed. She almost said something to that effect, and maybe she was old-fashioned, but she'd never been secure enough to make the first move. Especially with someone she respected as much as Garret. But perhaps it was for the best.

When the newspaper came out on Wednesday morning, as usual, Megan worried that, thanks to the small town rumor mill, it would be old news. And yet people kept coming into the office for newspapers, showing up even after they were completely out. And Arthur, following her directions, had printed twice as much as normal.

"That never happened before," Arthur said as he turned off the lights. It was only midday, but because of her dad's memorial service in the afternoon, they were quitting early.

"Francis Moore just told me that the whole town was out of papers, too," Barb said as she put the security code into the alarm system.

"Rory would be proud," Arthur told Megan. "And that editorial you wrote about him really got to me." The crusty old guy actually started to tear up.

"I'll say." Barb picked up her purse, pulling out a key ring. "I cried long and hard when I read it."

Arthur cleared his throat. "I guess we'll see you at the service later."

"Yeah." Megan nodded as they stepped outside. "Thanks again, you guys."

They all shared a group hug and then Megan got into her car and drove back to her dad's house. She'd been staying there since hearing the news that most of the Marco mob had been taken into custody with bails so high that no one had managed to get released as yet.

As she went into Dad's house, she had an imaginary conversation with him. "What do you think I should do?" she asked as she went into the kitchen to fix herself a bite of lunch. She stood by the kitchen window, looking out over the ocean, and felt such a sense of comfort and peace that she could almost imagine her dad's hand resting on her shoulder as the words *haste makes waste* went through her mind.

Yes, that sounded like Dad. But then she'd grown up hearing his adages. As a teenager she'd made fun of them. But now she liked them. So if haste made waste what was it that she was hurrying and how was it wasteful?

Selling the newspaper. Selling his house. She remembered what Garret had said to her, about how his grandmother was advised not to make any major decisions after her husband's death. Maybe it was better to wait.

She gazed out over the ocean, feeling the old connection that she'd loved so much as a girl, longing to go out in Dad's fishing boat one more time. Not that it was possible since it was probably out there at the bottom of the ocean somewhere. But even that brought a bit of comfort to her. It seemed right that Rory McCallister's boat had been put to rest like that. Her dad probably liked that.

Worn out from two long days of work, Megan

ate her lunch then sat down to relax. When she woke up, she realized she was now running late. Mad at herself for being late to her own dad's service, she tried not to speed into town. At least the tourists were gone now. It was nice to see the sweet little town returning to normal.

As she turned down the church's street, Megan didn't have high expectations about her dad's service. She was well aware that his opposition to the casino and a few other things had put him on some of the locals' hate lists. For all she knew, there would just be a handful here. And that was fine. But to her shock, the parking lot was full and she was forced to park several blocks away. Running to the church, she hoped that they hadn't started without her.

Garret was waiting for her at the front door. "Glad you made it," he said as he linked his arm in hers. "I told the pastor to wait."

"Thanks. I fell asleep."

"I tried your phone and was about to go looking for you," he said quietly as he led her to the front of the church.

The service was even better than she'd hoped for. Afterward, people greeted her, sharing sweet memories of Rory and expressing appreciation for today's paper. Their stories were truly heartwarming.

By the time she was leaving the church she felt

almost happy. Almost. But as Garret came over to walk with her, her happy meter tipped even more. "Thanks for your help," she said quietly.

"I made you a promise," Garret said as he walked her to her car.

"What's that?" She paused to unlock her door.

"I said I'd take you out to spread Rory's ashes in the ocean…if you like."

"Oh, yeah." She nodded eagerly then frowned. "But what about your boat?"

"I have another boat—a bigger one. It's the one I take on the ocean. The boat in the shop is only big enough for river fishing."

She felt a rush of joy. "I'd just been wishing I could go out on the ocean."

"Tomorrow is Fisherman's Thursday." His teal-blue eyes twinkled like the sea on a sunny day. "And the weather is supposed to be good. Although there's a storm system coming Friday."

"I'd love to go out."

"Great!"

As Garret got his boat ready on Thursday morning, he felt a mixture of anxiety and hope. Part of him was preparing for the worst. But another part of him was optimistic. He had made up his mind last night. No matter how it turned out, he was determined to tell Megan—once and for all—how he really felt about her. This would be a first for him. But then he'd never met a woman like Megan. And despite having only been reacquainted with her for a week, he knew that she was special. He honestly believed she was his soul mate. The question was—how did she feel? Today he would find out.

But not until they'd taken care of Rory's ashes. As he gave the chairs a wipe-down and moved some fishing junk out of the way, he wondered if he was pushing it. But he also knew that Megan had been planning to return to Seattle this weekend, maybe as soon as tomorrow. That left little time. And somehow, the idea of being out on the ocean together felt right. And he felt certain that Rory would approve.

Garret heard a cheerful greeting from the dock and looked up to see Megan waving. She had on her blue parka, which looked like it had been washed, as well as an old fishing hat that he felt certain he'd seen on Rory. In her hand was a small metal canister.

"Ahoy!" he called out as she came up to his boat.

"Nice little skiff you got here." She looked from bow to stern, giving it a nod of approval. "Impressive."

"Thanks." He grinned as he reached for her hand. "Your dad used to give me a bad time about having such a big fancy boat. But like I told him, it was my grandpa's. I just haven't had the heart to trade down." He helped her into the boat, slipping his arm around her waist as she landed—and wanting to keep it there.

"And why should you? This boat is absolutely beautiful." She ran her hand over the railing. "She's a jewel."

"And she can handle the ocean nicely, too." He leaned over to pull in a bumper from the stern area and, just like a seasoned sailor, Megan set down her canister of ashes then went for the other bumpers. Pulling them out of the water, she gave each one a firm shake then tucked it inside. Meanwhile, he untied the lines and started the engine and, just like that, they were on their way. It all felt so right. So much so that he wondered if he was deluded. Maybe this was a bad idea, after all. He glanced grimly at the canister now sitting on the dash. Maybe he was pushing it.

"What a perfect day," she declared as he headed downriver, observing the speed limit as he passed by other docks in town.

"Fisherman's Thursday," he said loudly to be heard over the engine and the slapping of the waves.

She let out a big sigh. "I feel like Dad's really with us."

He nodded. "I'd had similar thoughts."

"I've been thinking about him a lot these past few days," she said. "It's like I've finally had time to really do that."

"Yeah, you had a pretty busy few days when you first got here."

"I know. In a way it was good. It kind of helped me to get past the worst of the pain. It's like I can be happy for his life now and remember all the good times. You know?"

"Yeah, I get that."

"I mean, I still get sad. But not like I was. I was so devastated at first. And then it just got worse the more I learned about what was going on here. But now it sort of feels like his life had real purpose."

He agreed with her then continued to listen as she reminisced about Rory. It felt like she needed to talk. And he was relieved to hear her. As they passed beneath the bridge she told him about the first time Rory had taken her deep-sea fishing. "I was sick as a dog and Dad was so disappointed that I felt even worse. It took me a whole year before I went out again. But Dad had me take a seasick pill and eat the right kind of breakfast and I was just fine. Never been seasick since."

"You seem like a natural sailor," he said as he navigated the river between the jetties.

"And I've missed it," she confessed. "You'd

think I'd have been out since living in Seattle. And really, lots of people take boats out on the Sound. But I haven't been in a boat since the last time I went salmon fishing with Dad. And that was three and a half years ago." She shook her head with dismay. "I do regret that."

"Well, Rory would be pleased to see you out here today." He glanced at her. "Hold on, it might be a little rough crossing the bar. They said there might be some six-foot swells. But nothing to be concerned over in this boat."

"I feel perfectly safe." Even so she held on to the dash handle in front of her. "I think swells are fun."

He smiled as he gunned his engine. She was his kind of girl! Before long, they were in the open sea and when they reached the area where the coast guard had said Rory's boat had gone down, Garret slowed to a crawl and Megan unscrewed the lid to the canister.

"I know this isn't really you, Dad," she said as she leaned over the railing. "I know that you're with God in heaven. But it's symbolic of you." Her voice cracked with emotion. "Thank you for all you did for me. I love you, Dad. I always will." And then she poured the ashes out into the waves.

Garret wasn't sure what to do and so he continued aiming directly into the waves, which were actually getting a little bigger. Nothing dangerous, but maybe the predicted storm was coming sooner than predicted. Megan stood up straight, refastening the lid to the canister and setting it on the deck by her bag. "There," she said with satisfaction, wiping tears from her cheek. "It feels good to have that done."

Garret held out his left arm as he held on to the helm with his right hand. "Need a hug?"

She nodded with a trembling chin. "Yes, that'd be good." She came over to stand next to him and he securely held her with his left hand, giving her a sideways squeeze and holding her close. After a bit, he almost expected her to step away, but when she didn't, he thought maybe this was it—his big opportunity.

"Megan," he began slowly. "There's something I need to tell you."

She looked up at him with troubled eyes. "Is something wrong?"

"No. I mean, I hope not." He swallowed hard, wondering why this was so difficult. "Megan, you've come to mean a lot to me this past week."

She just nodded. "Yeah, I feel the same way."

"It kind of took me by surprise," he confessed. "But it was a good surprise."

She nodded again, and now he felt encouraged.

"Megan," he said firmly, "you walked into my life a week ago and turned it upside down.

And now you plan to leave it. But I'm begging you to rethink that."

"Rethink that?" She studied him closely with a hint of a smile playing on her lips.

"Megan McCallister, I love you," he declared. "And although I know it might seem sudden, I am not willing to part with you. I'm asking you to stay here, Megan. Stay here in Cape Perpetua and please consider marrying me."

She blinked. "Is this a proposal?"

He was shocked at himself. He had planned to declare his love for her. As much as he wanted to marry her, he hadn't meant to bowl her over with a premature proposal. And yet he had done just that and it was too late to take it back. Not that he wanted to. But at the same time, he didn't want to scare her away, either. But he was in too deep and had no plans to back off. Garret nodded his head firmly. "Yes. I'm sorry for making such a giant leap. But it is a proposal."

Megan let out a whoop of delight as she threw both arms around his neck. "Garret Larsson, I love you, too. It feels like I've loved you for ages!"

"Really?" He stared at her with wonder. "You're sure?"

"Absolutely, positively." She grinned at him, knowing how pleased Dad would be to know that she would take over the newspaper. But better than that was knowing Garret was about to kiss her.

Suddenly they were kissing—so long and so passionately that Garret forgot to keep steering the boat into the waves.

"Easy there, Captain." Megan placed her hand on the helm opposite his, gently helping to steer the boat back into the waves.

He laughed. "I needed a first mate."

"Well, here I am.

* * * * *

Dear Reader,

Thanks for sharing in the adventure of *Against the Tide*. Although this book is set in a fictional town, it is strikingly similar to where our beach cabin was located—on the central Oregon coast. The beautiful river, picturesque docks, massive jetties and miles of sand dunes...all were inspired by a very real place called Florence, Oregon.

Unfortunately, we had to sell our beach cabin last year—while I was writing this very book!— but the sweet memories of that area remain with us, and we still go back to visit our favorite town whenever we get a hankering for the Oregon coast.

As many of my readers know, I love beachside settings for storytelling. My first novel was set by the ocean, as well as my previous suspense romance, *No One to Trust*. And, of course, I will continue to use a seaside backdrop for some of my future books. Because whether it's to enhance romance or intrigue or history, I think coastal towns have a lot to offer.

Anyway, I hope you enjoyed this book. Thank you again for reading!

Blessings!
Melody Carlson

LARGER-PRINT BOOKS!

GET 2 FREE LARGER-PRINT NOVELS PLUS 2 FREE MYSTERY GIFTS

Love Inspired®

Larger-print novels are now available...

YES! Please send me 2 FREE LARGER-PRINT Love Inspired® novels and my 2 FREE mystery gifts (gifts are worth about $10). After receiving them, if I don't wish to receive any more books, I can return the shipping statement marked "cancel." If I don't cancel, I will receive 6 brand-new novels every month and be billed just $5.49 per book in the U.S. or $5.99 per book in Canada. That's a savings of at least 19% off the cover price. It's quite a bargain! Shipping and handling is just 50¢ per book in the U.S. and 75¢ per book in Canada.* I understand that accepting the 2 free books and gifts places me under no obligation to buy anything. I can always return a shipment and cancel at any time. Even if I never buy another book, the two free books and gifts are mine to keep forever.

122/322 IDN GH6D

Name _____ (PLEASE PRINT)

Address _____ Apt. #

City _____ State/Prov. _____ Zip/Postal Code

Signature (if under 18, a parent or guardian must sign)

Mail to the **Reader Service:**
IN U.S.A.: P.O. Box 1867, Buffalo, NY 14240-1867
IN CANADA: P.O. Box 609, Fort Erie, Ontario L2A 5X3

**Are you a current subscriber to Love Inspired® books
and want to receive the larger-print edition?
Call 1-800-873-8635 or visit www.ReaderService.com.**

* Terms and prices subject to change without notice. Prices do not include applicable taxes. Sales tax applicable in N.Y. Canadian residents will be charged applicable taxes. Offer not valid in Quebec. This offer is limited to one order per household. Not valid to current subscribers to Love Inspired Larger-Print books. All orders subject to credit approval. Credit or debit balances in a customer's account(s) may be offset by any other outstanding balance owed by or to the customer. Please allow 4 to 6 weeks for delivery. Offer available while quantities last.

Your Privacy—The Reader Service is committed to protecting your privacy. Our Privacy Policy is available online at www.ReaderService.com or upon request from the Reader Service.

We make a portion of our mailing list available to reputable third parties that offer products we believe may interest you. If you prefer that we not exchange your name with third parties, or if you wish to clarify or modify your communication preferences, please visit us at www.ReaderService.com/consumerschoice or write to us at Reader Service Preference Service, P.O. Box 9062, Buffalo, NY 14240-9062. Include your complete name and address.

LILP15